APPRECIATIONS

APPRECIATIONS

WITH AN ESSAY ON STYLE

BY

WALTER PATER

FELLOW OF BRASENOSE COLLEGE

Northwestern University Press
Evanston, Illinois

820.9
P

Printed and bound in the United States of America.

Published in 1987 by Northwestern University Press,
1735 Benson Avenue, Evanston, IL 60201.

First published in 1889 by Macmillian and Co., London.

TO THE MEMORY OF MY BROTHER

WILLIAM THOMPSON PATER

WHO QUITTED A USEFUL AND HAPPY LIFE

SUNDAY APRIL 24 1887

REQUIEM ETERNAM DONA EI DOMINE

ET LUX PERPETUA LUCEAT EI

P. V

CONTENTS

STYLE

Since all progress of mind consists for the most part in differentiation, in the resolution of an obscure and complex object into its component aspects, it is surely the stupidest of losses to confuse things which right reason has put asunder, to lose the sense of achieved distinctions, the distinction between poetry and prose, for instance, or, to speak more exactly, between the laws and characteristic excellences of verse and prose composition. On the other hand, those who have dwelt most emphatically on the distinction between prose and verse, prose and poetry, may sometimes have been tempted to limit the proper functions of prose too narrowly; and this again is at least false economy, as being, in effect, the renunciation of a certain means or faculty, in a world where after all we must needs make the most of things. Critical efforts to limit art *a priori*, by anticipations regarding the natural incapacity of the material with which this or that artist works, as the sculptor with solid form, or the prose-writer with the ordinary

5

language of men, are always liable to be discredited by the facts of artistic production ; and
while prose is actually found to be a coloured
thing with Bacon, picturesque with Livy and
Carlyle, musical with Cicero and Newman,
mystical and intimate with Plato and Michelet
and Sir Thomas Browne, exalted or florid, it may
be, with Milton and Taylor, it will be useless to
protest that it can be nothing at all, except something very tamely and narrowly confined to
mainly practical ends—a kind of " good round-
hand ; " as useless as the protest that poetry
might not touch prosaic subjects as with Wordsworth, or an abstruse matter as with Browning,
or treat contemporary life nobly as with Tennyson. In subordination to one essential beauty
in all good literary style, in all literature as a
fine art, as there are many beauties of poetry so
the beauties of prose are many, and it is the
business of criticism to estimate them as such ;
as it is good in the criticism of verse to look for
those hard, logical, and quasi-prosaic excellences
which that too has, or needs. To find in the
poem, amid the flowers, the allusions, the mixed
perspectives, of *Lycidas* for instance, the thought,
the logical structure :—how wholesome ! how
delightful ! as to identify in prose what we call
the poetry, the imaginative power, not treating
it as out of place and a kind of vagrant intruder,
but by way of an estimate of its rights, that is,
of its achieved powers, there.

STYLE

Dryden, with the characteristic instinct of his age, loved to emphasise the distinction between poetry and prose, the protest against their confusion with each other, coming with somewhat diminished effect from one whose poetry was so prosaic. In truth, his sense of prosaic excellence affected his verse rather than his prose, which is not only fervid, richly figured, poetic, as we say, but vitiated, all unconsciously, by many a scanning line. Setting up correctness, that humble merit of prose, as the central literary excellence, he is really a less correct writer than he may seem, still with an imperfect mastery of the relative pronoun. It might have been foreseen that, in the rotations of mind, the province of poetry in prose would find its assertor ; and, a century after Dryden, amid very different intellectual needs, and with the need therefore of great modifications in literary form, the range of the poetic force in literature was effectively enlarged by Wordsworth. The true distinction between prose and poetry he regarded as the almost technical or accidental one of the absence or presence of metrical beauty, or, say ! metrical restraint ; and for him the opposition came to be between verse and prose of course ; but, as the essential dichotomy in this matter, between imaginative and unimaginative writing, parallel to De Quincey's distinction between " the literature of power and the literature of knowledge," in the former of which the composer gives us not fact, but his peculiar sense of fact, whether past or present.

Dismissing then, under sanction of Wordsworth, that harsher opposition of poetry to prose, as savouring in fact of the arbitrary psychology of the last century, and with it the prejudice that there can be but one only beauty of prose style, I propose here to point out certain qualities of all literature as a fine art, which, if they apply to the literature of fact, apply still more to the literature of the imaginative sense of fact, while they apply indifferently to verse and prose, so far as either is really imaginative—certain conditions of true art in both alike, which conditions may also contain in them the secret of the proper discrimination and guardianship of the peculiar excellences of either.

The line between fact and something quite different from external fact is, indeed, hard to draw. In Pascal, for instance, in the persuasive writers generally, how difficult to define the point where, from time to time, argument which, if it is to be worth anything at all, must consist of facts or groups of facts, becomes a pleading— a theorem no longer, but essentially an appeal to the reader to catch the writer's spirit, to think with him, if one can or will—an expression no longer of fact but of his sense of it, his peculiar intuition of a world, prospective, or discerned below the faulty conditions of the present, in either case changed somewhat from the actual world. In science, on the other hand, in history so far as it conforms to scientific rule, we have a literary domain where the imagination may be thought to be always an intruder. And as, in all science, the functions of literature reduce themselves eventually to the transcribing of fact, so all the excellences of literary form in regard to science are reducible to various kinds of pains-taking ; this good quality being involved in all " skilled work " whatever, in the drafting of an act of parliament, as in sewing. Yet here again, the writer's sense of fact, in history especially, and in all those complex subjects which do but lie on the borders of science, will still take the place of fact, in various degrees. Your historian, for instance, with absolutely truthful intention, amid the multitude of facts presented to him must needs select, and in selecting assert something of his own humour, something that comes not of the world without but of a vision within. So Gibbon moulds his unwieldy material to a preconceived view. Livy, Tacitus, Michelet, moving full of poignant sensibility amid the records of the past, each, after his own sense, modifies—who can tell where and to what degree ?—and becomes something else than a transcriber ; each, as he thus modifies, passing into the domain of art proper. For just in pro-portion as the writer's aim, consciously or un-consciously, comes to be the transcribing, not of the world, not of mere fact, but of his sense of it, he becomes an artist, his work *fine* art ; and good art (as I hope ultimately to show) in proportion to the truth of his presentment of that sense ; as in those humbler or plainer functions of literature also, truth—truth to bare fact, there—is the essence of such artistic quality as they may have. Truth ! there can be no merit, no craft at all, without that. And further, all beauty is in the long run only *fineness* of truth, or what we call expression, the finer accommodation of speech to that vision within.

—The transcript of his sense of fact rather than the fact, as being preferable, pleasanter, more beautiful to the writer himself. In literature, as in every other product of human skill, in the moulding of a bell or a platter for instance, wherever this sense asserts itself, wherever the producer so modifies his work as, over and above its primary use or intention, to make it pleasing (to himself, of course, in the first instance) there, " fine " as opposed to merely serviceable art, exists. Literary art, that is, like all art which is in any way imitative or reproductive of fact— form, or colour, or incident—is the representation of such fact as connected with soul, of a specific personality, in its preferences, its volition and power.

Such is the matter of imaginative or artistic literature—this transcript, not of mere fact, but of fact in its infinite variety, as modified by human preference in all its infinitely varied

forms. It will be good literary art not because
it is brilliant or sober, or rich, or impulsive, or
severe, but just in proportion as its representation
of that sense, that soul-fact, is true, verse being
only one department of such literature, and
imaginative prose, it may be thought, being the
special art of the modern world. That imaginative prose should be the special and opportune
art of the modern world results from two important facts about the latter : first, the chaotic
variety and complexity of its interests, making
the intellectual issue, the really master currents
of the present time incalculable —a condition of
mind little susceptible of the restraint proper to
verse form, so that the most characteristic verse
of the nineteenth century has been lawless verse ;
and secondly, an all-pervading naturalism, a
curiosity about everything whatever as it really
is, involving a certain humility of attitude,
cognate to what must, after all, be the less
ambitious form of literature. And prose thus
asserting itself as the special and privileged
artistic faculty of the present day, will be, however critics may try to narrow its scope, as varied
in its excellence as humanity itself reflecting on
the facts of its latest experience—an instrument
of many stops, meditative, observant, descriptive,
eloquent, analytic, plaintive, fervid. Its beauties
will be not exclusively " pedestrian " : it will
exert, in due measure, all the varied charms of
poetry, down to the rhythm which, as in Cicero,

or Michelet, or Newman, at their best, gives its musical value to every syllable.[1] The literary artist is of necessity a scholar, and in what he proposes to do will have in mind, first of all, the scholar and the scholarly conscience—the male conscience in this matter, as we must think it, under a system of education which still to so large an extent limits real scholarship to men. In his self-criticism, he supposes always that sort of reader who will go (full of eyes) warily, considerately, though without consideration for him, over the ground which the female conscience traverses so lightly, so amiably. For the material in which he works is no more a creation of his own than the sculptor's marble. Product of a myriad various minds and contending tongues, compact of obscure and minute association, a language has its own abundant and often recondite laws, in the habitual and summary recognition of which scholarship consists. A writer, full of a matter he is before all things anxious to express, may think of those laws, the limitations of vocabulary, structure, and the like, as a restriction, but if a

[1] Mr. Saintsbury, in his *Specimens of English Prose, from Malory to Macaulay*, has succeeded in tracing, through successive English prose-writers, the tradition of that severer beauty in them, of which this admirable scholar of our literature is known to be a lover. *English Prose, from Mandeville to Thackeray*, more recently "chosen and edited" by a younger scholar, Mr. Arthur Galton, of New College, Oxford, a lover of our literature at once enthusiastic and discreet, aims at a more various illustration of the eloquent powers of English prose, and is a delightful companion.

real artist will find in them an opportunity. His punctilious observance of the proprieties of his medium will diffuse through all he writes a general air of sensibility, of refined usage. *Exclusiones debitæ naturæ*—the exclusions, or rejections, which nature demands—we know how large a part these play, according to Bacon, in the science of nature. In a somewhat changed sense, we might say that the art of the scholar is summed up in the observance of those rejections demanded by the nature of his medium, the material he must use. Alive to the value of an atmosphere in which every term finds its utmost degree of expression, and with all the jealousy of a lover of words, he will resist a constant tendency on the part of the majority of those who use them to efface the distinctions of language, the facility of writers often reinforcing in this respect the work of the vulgar. He will feel the obligation not of the laws only, but of those affinities, avoidances, those mere preferences, of his language, which through the associations of literary history have become a part of its nature, prescribing the rejection of many a neology, many a license, many a gipsy phrase which might present itself as actually expressive. His appeal, again, is to the scholar, who has great experience in literature, and will show no favour to short-cuts, or hackneyed illustration, or an affectation of learning designed for the unlearned. Hence a contention, a sense of self-restraint and renunciation, having for the susceptible reader the effect of a challenge for minute consideration ; the attention of the writer, in every minutest detail, being a pledge that it is worth the reader's while to be attentive too, that the writer is dealing scrupulously with his instrument, and therefore, indirectly, with the reader himself also, that he has the science of the instrument he plays on, perhaps, after all, with a freedom which in such case will be the freedom of a master.

For meanwhile, braced only by those restraints, he is really vindicating his liberty in the making of a vocabulary, an entire system of composition, for himself, his own true manner ; and when we speak of the manner of a true master we mean what is essential in his art. Pedantry being only the scholarship of *le cuistre* (we have no English equivalent) he is no pedant, and does but show his intelligence of the rules of language in his freedoms with it, addition or expansion, which like the spontaneities of manner in a well-bred person will still further illustrate good taste. —The right vocabulary ! Translators have not invariably seen how all-important that is in the work of translation, driving for the most part at idiom or construction ; whereas, if the original be first-rate, one's first care should be with its elementary particles, Plato, for instance, being often reproducible by an exact following, with no variation in structure, of word after word, as the pencil follows a drawing under tracing-paper, so only each word or syllable be not of false colour, to change my illustration a little.

Well ! that is because any writer worth translating at all has winnowed and searched through his vocabulary, is conscious of the words he would select in systematic reading of a dictionary, and still more of the words he would reject were the dictionary other than Johnson's ; and doing this with his peculiar sense of the world ever in view, in search of an instrument for the adequate expression of that, he begets a vocabulary faithful to the colouring of his own spirit, and in the strictest sense original. That living authority which language needs lies, in truth, in its scholars, who recognising always that every language possesses a genius, a very fastidious genius, of its own, expand at once and purify its very elements, which must needs change along with the changing thoughts of living people. Ninety years ago, for instance, great mental force, certainly, was needed by Wordsworth, to break through the consecrated poetic associations of a century, and speak the language that was his, that was to become in a measure the language of the next generation. But he did it with the tact of a scholar also. English, for a quarter of a century past, has been assimilating the phraseology of pictorial art ; for half a century, the phraseology of the great German metaphysical movement of eighty years ago ; in part also the language of mystical theology : and none but pedants will regret a great consequent increase of its resources. For many years to come its enterprise may well lie in the naturalisation of the vocabulary of science, so only it be under the eye of a sensitive scholarship—in a liberal naturalisation of the ideas of science too, for after all the chief stimulus of good style is to possess a full, rich, complex matter to grapple with. The literary artist, therefore, will be well aware of physical science ; science also attaining, in its turn, its true literary ideal. And then, as the scholar is nothing without the historic sense, he will be apt to restore not really obsolete or really worn-out words, but the finer edge of words still in use : *ascertain, communicate, discover*— words like these it has been part of our "business" to misuse. And still, as language was made for man, he will be no authority for correctnesses which, limiting freedom of utterance, were yet but accidents in their origin ; as if one vowed not to say "*its*," which ought to have been in Shakespeare ; "*his*" and "*hers*," for inanimate objects, being but a barbarous and really inexpressive survival. Yet we have known many things like this. Racy Saxon monosyllables, close to us as touch and sight, he will intermix readily with those long, savoursome, Latin words, rich in "second intention." In this late day certainly, no critical process can be conducted reasonably without eclecticism. Of such eclecticism we have a justifying example in one of the first poets of our time. How illustrative of monosyllabic effect, of sonorous Latin, of the phraseology of science, of metaphysic, of colloquialism even, are the writings of Tennyson ; yet with what a fine, fastidious scholarship throughout!

A scholar writing for the scholarly, he will of course leave something to the willing intelligence of his reader. " To go preach to the first passer-by," says Montaigne, " to become tutor to the ignorance of the first I meet, is a thing I abhor ; " a thing, in fact, naturally distressing to the scholar, who will therefore ever be shy of offering uncomplimentary assistance to the reader's wit. To really strenuous minds there is a pleasurable stimulus in the challenge for a continuous effort on their part, to be rewarded by securer and more intimate grasp of the author's sense. Self-restraint, a skilful economy of means, *ascêsis*, that too has a beauty of its own ; and for the reader supposed there will be an æsthetic satisfaction in that frugal closeness of style which makes the most of a word, in the exaction from every sentence of a precise relief, in the just spacing out of word to thought, in the logically filled space connected always with the delightful sense of difficulty overcome.

Different classes of persons, at different times, make, of course, very various demands upon literature. Still, scholars, I suppose, and not only scholars, but all disinterested lovers of books, will always look to it, as to all other fine art, for a refuge, a sort of cloistral refuge, from a certain vulgarity in the actual world. A perfect poem like *Lycidas*, a perfect fiction like *Esmond*, the perfect handling of a theory like Newman's *Idea of a University*, has for them something of the uses of a religious "retreat." Here, then, with a view to the central need of a select few, those "men of a finer thread" who have formed and maintain the literary ideal, everything, every component element, will have undergone exact trial, and, above all, there will be no uncharacteristic or tarnished or vulgar decoration, permissible ornament being for the most part structural, or necessary. As the painter in his picture, so the artist in his book, aims at the production by honourable artifice of a peculiar atmosphere. "The artist," says Schiller, "may be known rather by what he *omits*"; and in literature, too, the true artist may be best recognised by his tact of omission. For to the grave reader words too are grave; and the ornamental word, the figure, the accessory form or colour or reference, is rarely content to die to thought precisely at the right moment, but will inevitably linger awhile, stirring a long "brain-wave" behind it of perhaps quite alien associations.

Just there, it may be, is the detrimental tendency of the sort of scholarly attentiveness of mind I am recommending. But the true artist allows for it. He will remember that, as the very word ornament indicates what is in itself non-essential, so the " one beauty " of all literary style is of its very essence, and independent, in prose and verse alike, of all removable decoration ; that it may exist in its fullest lustre, as in Flaubert's *Madame Bovary*, for instance, or in Stendhal's *Le Rouge et Le Noir*, in a composition utterly unadorned, with hardly a single suggestion of visibly beautiful things. Parallel, allusion, the allusive way generally, the flowers in the garden :—he knows the narcotic force of these upon the negligent intelligence to which any *diversion*, literally, is welcome, any vagrant intruder, because one can go wandering away with it from the immediate subject. Jealous, if he have a really quickening motive within, of all that does not hold directly to that, of the facile, the otiose, he will never depart from the strictly pedestrian process, unless he gains a ponderable something thereby. Even assured of its congruity, he will still question its serviceableness. Is it worth while, can we afford, to attend to just that, to just that figure or literary reference, just then ?—Surplusage ! he will dread that, as the runner on his muscles. For in truth all art does but consist in the removal of surplusage, from the last finish of the gem-engraver blowing away the last particle of invisible dust, back to the earliest divination of the finished work to be, lying somewhere, according to Michelangelo's fancy, in the rough-hewn block of stone.

And what applies to figure or flower must be understood of all other accidental or removable ornaments of writing whatever ; and not of specific ornament only, but of all that latent colour and imagery which language as such carries in it. A lover of words for their own sake, to whom nothing about them is unimportant, a minute and constant observer of their physiognomy, he will be on the alert not only for obviously mixed metaphors of course, but for the metaphor that is mixed in all our speech, though a rapid use may involve no cognition of it. Currently recognising the incident, the colour, the physical elements or particles in words like *absorb*, *consider*, *extract*, to take the first that occur, he will avail himself of them, as further adding to the resources of expression. The elementary particles of language will be realised as colour and light and shade through his scholarly living in the full sense of them. Still opposing the constant degradation of language by those who use it carelessly, he will not treat coloured glass as if it were clear ; and while half the world is using figure unconsciously, will be fully aware not only of all that latent figurative texture in speech, but of the vague, lazy, half-formed personification —a rhetoric, depressing, and worse than nothing, because it has no really rhetorical motive—which plays so large a part there, and, as in the case of more ostentatious ornament, scrupulously exact of it, from syllable to syllable, its precise value.

So far I have been speaking of certain conditions of the literary art arising out of the medium or material in or upon which it works, the essential qualities of language and its aptitudes for contingent ornamentation, matters which define scholarship as science and good taste respectively. They are both subservient to a more intimate quality of good style : more intimate, as coming nearer to the artist himself. The otiose, the facile, surplusage : why are these abhorrent to the true literary artist, except because, in literary as in all other art, structure is all-important, felt, or painfully missed, everywhere ?—that architectural conception of work, which foresees the end in the beginning and never loses sight of it, and in every part is conscious of all the rest, till the last sentence does but, with undiminished vigour, unfold and justify the first—a condition of literary art, which, in contradistinction to another quality of the artist himself, to be spoken of later, I shall call the necessity of *mind* in style.

An acute philosophical writer, the late Dean Mansel (a writer whose works illustrate the literary beauty there may be in closeness, and with obvious repression or economy of a fine rhetorical gift) wrote a book, of fascinating precision in a very obscure subject, to show that all the technical laws of logic are but means of securing, in each and all of its apprehensions, the unity, the strict identity with itself, of the apprehending mind. All the laws of good writing aim at a similar unity or identity of the mind in all the processes by which the word is associated to its import. The term is right, and has its essential beauty, when it becomes, in a manner, what it signifies, as with the names of simple sensations. To give the phrase, the sentence, the structural member, the entire composition, song, or essay, a similar unity with its subject and with itself:—style is in the right way when it tends towards that. All depends upon the original unity, the vital wholeness and identity, of the initiatory apprehension or view. So much is true of all art, which therefore requires always its logic, its comprehensive reason—insight, foresight, retrospect, in simultaneous action—true, most of all, of the literary art, as being of all the arts most closely cognate to the abstract intelligence. Such logical coherency may be evidenced not merely in the lines of composition as a whole, but in the choice of a single word, while it by no means interferes with, but may even prescribe, much variety, in the building of the sentence for instance, or in the manner, argumentative, descriptive, discursive, of this or that part or member of the entire design. The blithe, crisp sentence, decisive as a child's expression of its needs, may alternate with the long-contending, victoriously intricate sentence ; the sentence, born with the integrity of a single word, relieving the sort of sentence in which, if you look closely, you can see much contrivance, much adjustment, to bring a highly qualified matter into compass at one view. For the literary architecture, if it is to be rich and expressive, involves not only foresight of the end in the beginning, but also development or growth of design, in the process of execution, with many irregularities, surprises, and afterthoughts ; the contingent as well as the necessary being subsumed under the unity of the whole. As truly, to the lack of such architectural design, of a single, almost visual, image, vigorously informing an entire, perhaps very intricate, composition, which shall be austere, ornate, argumentative, fanciful, yet true from first to last to that vision within, may be attributed those weaknesses of conscious or unconscious repetition of word, phrase, motive, or member of the whole matter, indicating, as Flaubert was aware, an original structure in thought not organically complete. With such foresight, the actual conclusion will most often get itself written out of hand, before, in the more obvious sense, the work is finished. With some strong and leading sense of the world, the tight hold of which secures true *composition* and not mere loose accretion, the literary artist, I suppose, goes on considerately, setting joint to joint, sustained by yet restraining the productive ardour, retracing the negligences of his first sketch, repeating his steps only that he may give the reader a sense of secure and restful progress, readjusting mere assonances even, that they may soothe the reader, or at least not interrupt him on his way ; and then, somewhere before the end comes, is burdened, inspired, with his conclusion, and betimes delivered of it, leaving off, not in weariness and because he finds *himself* at an end, but in all the freshness of volition. His work now structurally complete, with all the accumulating effect of secondary shades of meaning, he finishes the whole up to the just proportion of that ante-penultimate conclusion, and all becomes expressive. The house he has built is rather a body he has informed. And so it happens, to its greater credit, that the better interest even of a narrative to be recounted, a story to be told, will often be in its second reading. And though there are instances of great writers who have been no artists, an unconscious tact sometimes directing work in which we may detect, very pleasurably, many of the effects of conscious art, yet one of the greatest pleasures of really good prose literature is in the critical tracing out of that conscious artistic structure, and the pervading sense of it as we read. Yet of poetic literature too ; for, in truth, the kind of constructive intelligence here supposed is one of the forms of the imagination.

That is the special function of mind, in style. Mind and soul :—hard to ascertain philosophically, the distinction is real enough practically, for they often interfere, are sometimes in conflict, with each other. Blake, in the last century, is an instance of preponderating soul, embarrassed, at a loss, in an era of preponderating mind. As a quality of style, at all events, soul is a fact, in certain writers—the way they have of absorbing language, of attracting it into the peculiar spirit they are of, with a subtlety which makes the actual result seem like some inexplicable inspiration. By mind, the literary artist reaches us, through static and objective indications of design in his work, legible to all. By soul, he reaches us, somewhat capriciously perhaps, one and not another, through vagrant sympathy and a kind of immediate contact. Mind we cannot choose but approve where we recognise it ; soul may repel us, not because we misunderstand it. The way in which theological interests sometimes avail themselves of language is perhaps the best illustration of the force I mean to indicate generally in literature, by the word *soul*. Ardent religious persuasion may exist, may make its way, without finding any equivalent heat in language : or, again, it may enkindle

APPRECIATIONS

words to various degrees, and when it really
takes hold of them doubles its force. Religious
history presents many remarkable instances in
which, through no mere phrase-worship, an
unconscious literary tact has, for the sensitive,
laid open a privileged pathway from one to
another. "The altar-fire," people say, "has
touched those lips!" The Vulgate, the English
Bible, the English Prayer-Book, the writings of
Swedenborg, the Tracts for the Times :—there,
we have instances of widely different and largely
diffused phases of religious feeling in operation
as soul in style. But something of the same
kind acts with similar power in certain writers
of quite other than theological literature, on
behalf of some wholly personal and peculiar
sense of theirs. Most easily illustrated by
theological literature, this quality lends to
profane writers a kind of religious influence.
At their best, these writers become, as we say
sometimes, "prophets"; such character depending on the effect not merely of their matter, but
of their matter as allied to, in "electric affinity"
with, peculiar form, and working in all cases by
an immediate sympathetic contact, on which
account it is that it may be called soul, as
opposed to mind, in style. And this too is
a faculty of choosing and rejecting what is
congruous or otherwise, with a drift towards
unity—unity of atmosphere here, as there of
design—soul securing colour (or perfume, might

26

we say ?) as mind secures form, the latter being essentially finite, the former vague or infinite, as the influence of a living person is practically infinite. There are some to whom nothing has any real interest, or real meaning, except as operative in a given person ; and it is they who best appreciate the quality of soul in literary art. They seem to know a *person*, in a book, and make way by intuition : yet, although they thus enjoy the completeness of a personal information, it is still a characteristic of soul, in this sense of the word, that it does but suggest what can never be uttered, not as being different from, or more obscure than, what actually gets said, but as containing that plenary substance of which there is only one phase or facet in what is there expressed.

If all high things have their martyrs, Gustave Flaubert might perhaps rank as the martyr of literary style. In his printed correspondence, a curious series of letters, written in his twenty-fifth year, records what seems to have been his one other passion—a series of letters which, with its fine casuistries, its firmly repressed anguish, its tone of harmonious grey, and the sense of disillusion in which the whole matter ends, might have been, a few slight changes supposed, one of his own fictions. Writing to Madame X. certainly he does display, by "taking thought" mainly, by constant and delicate pondering, as in his love for literature, a heart really moved, but still more, and as the pledge of that emotion, a loyalty to his work. Madame X., too, is a literary artist, and the best gifts he can send her are precepts of perfection in art, counsels for the effectual pursuit of that better love. In his love-letters it is the pains and pleasures of art he insists on, its solaces : he communicates secrets, reproves, encourages, with a view to that. Whether the lady was dissatisfied with such divided or indirect service, the reader is not enabled to see ; but sees that, on Flaubert's part at least, a living person could be no rival of what was, from first to last, his leading passion, a somewhat solitary and exclusive one.

I must scold you (he writes) for one thing, which shocks, scandalises me, the small concern, namely, you show for art just now. As regards glory be it so : there, I approve. But for art !—the one thing in life that is good and real—can you compare with it an earthly love ?—prefer the adoration of a relative beauty to the *cultus* of the true beauty ? Well ! I tell you the truth. That is the one thing good in me : the one thing I have, to me estimable. For yourself, you blend with the beautiful a heap of alien things, the useful, the agreeable, what not ?—

The only way not to be unhappy is to shut yourself up in art, and count everything else as nothing. Pride takes the place of all beside when it is established on a large basis. Work ! God wills it. That, it seems to me, is clear.—

I am reading over again the *Æneid*, certain verses of which I repeat to myself to satiety. There are phrases there which stay in one's head, by which I find myself beset, as with those musical airs which are for ever returning, and cause you pain, you love them so much. I observe that I no longer laugh much, and am no longer depressed. I am ripe. You talk of my serenity, and envy me. It may well surprise you. Sick, irritated, the prey a thousand times a day of cruel pain, I continue my labour like a true working-man, who, with sleeves turned up, in the sweat of his brow, beats away at his anvil, never troubling himself whether it rains or blows, for hail or thunder. I was not like that formerly. The change has taken place naturally, though my will has counted for something in the matter.—

Those who write in good style are sometimes accused of a neglect of ideas, and of the moral end, as if the end of the physician were something else than healing, of the painter than painting—as if the end of art were not, before all else, the beautiful.

What, then, did Flaubert understand by beauty, in the art he pursued with so much fervour, with so much self-command? Let us hear a sympathetic commentator :—

Possessed of an absolute belief that there exists but one way of expressing one thing, one word to call it by, one adjective to qualify, one verb to animate it, he gave himself to super-human labour for the discovery, in every phrase, of that word, that verb, that epithet. In this way, he believed in some mysterious harmony of expression, and when a true word seemed to him to lack euphony still went on seeking another, with invincible patience, certain that he had not yet got hold of the *unique* word. . . . A thousand preoccupations would beset him at the same moment, always with this desperate certitude fixed in his spirit : Among all the expressions in the world, all forms and turns ·of expression, there is but one—one form, one mode—to express what I want to say.

The one word for the one thing, the one thought, amid the multitude of words, terms, that might just do : the problem of style was there !—the unique word, phrase, sentence, paragraph, essay, or song, absolutely proper to the single mental presentation or vision within.

APPRECIATIONS

In that perfect justice, over and above the many contingent and removable beauties with which beautiful style may charm us, but which it can exist without, independent of them yet dexterously availing itself of them, omnipresent in good work, in function at every point, from single epithets to the rhythm of a whole book, lay the specific, indispensable, very intellectual, beauty of literature, the possibility of which constitutes it a fine art.

One seems to detect the influence of a philosophic idea there, the idea of a natural economy, of some pre-existent adaptation, between a relative, somewhere in the world of thought, and its correlative, somewhere in the world of language—both alike, rather, somewhere in the mind of the artist, desiderative, expectant, inventive—meeting each other with the readiness of " soul and body reunited," in Blake's rapturous design ; and, in fact, Flaubert was fond of giving his theory philosophical expression.—

There are no beautiful thoughts (he would say) without beautiful forms, and conversely. As it is impossible to extract from a physical body the qualities which really constitute it— colour, extension, and the like—without reducing it to a hollow abstraction, in a word, without destroying it ; just so it is impossible to detach the form from the idea, for the idea only exists by virtue of the form.

All the recognised flowers, the removable ornaments of literature (including harmony and ease in reading aloud, very carefully considered

by him) counted, certainly ; for these too are
part of the actual value of what one says. But
still, after all, with Flaubert, the search, the
unwearied research, was not for the smooth, or
winsome, or forcible word, as such, as with false
Ciceronians, but quite simply and honestly, for
the word's adjustment to its meaning. The first
condition of this must be, of course, to know
yourself, to have ascertained your own sense
exactly. Then, if we suppose an artist, he says
to the reader,—I want you to see precisely what
I see. Into the mind sensitive to "form," a
flood of random sounds, colours, incidents, is ever
penetrating from the world without, to become,
by sympathetic selection, a part of its very structure, and, in turn, the visible vesture and expression of that other world it sees so steadily within,
nay, already with a partial conformity thereto,
to be refined, enlarged, corrected, at a hundred
points ; and it is just there, just at those doubtful
points that the function of style, as tact or taste,
intervenes. The unique term will come more
quickly to one than another, at one time than
another, according also to the kind of matter in
question. Quickness and slowness, ease and
closeness alike, have nothing to do with the
artistic character of the true word found at last.
As there is a charm of ease, so there is also a
special charm in the signs of discovery, of effort
and contention towards a due end, as so often
with Flaubert himself—in the style which has

been pliant, as only obstinate, durable metal can be, to the inherent perplexities and recusancy of a certain difficult thought. If Flaubert had not told us, perhaps we should never have guessed how tardy and painful his own procedure really was, and after reading his confession may think that his almost endless hesitation had much to do with diseased nerves. Often, perhaps, the felicity supposed will be the product of a happier, a more exuberant nature than Flaubert's. Aggravated, certainly, by a morbid physical condition, that anxiety in " seeking the phrase," which gathered all the other small *ennuis* of a really quiet existence into a kind of battle, was connected with his lifelong contention against facile poetry, facile art—art, facile and flimsy ; and what constitutes the true artist is not the slowness or quickness of the process, but the absolute success of the result. As with those labourers in the parable, the prize is independent of the mere length of the actual day's work. " You talk," he writes, odd, trying lover, to Madame X.—

" You talk of the exclusiveness of my literary tastes. That might have enabled you to divine what kind of a person I am in the matter of love. I grow so hard to please as a literary artist, that I am driven to despair. I shall end by not writing another line."

" Happy," he cries, in a moment of discouragement at that patient labour, which for him, certainly, was the condition of a great success—

STYLE

Happy those who have no doubts of themselves! who lengthen out, as the pen runs on, all that flows forth from their brains. As for me, I hesitate, I disappoint myself, turn round upon myself in despite : my taste is augmented in proportion as my natural vigour decreases, and I afflict my soul over some dubious word out of all proportion to the pleasure I get from a whole page of good writing. One would have to live two centuries to attain a true idea of any matter whatever. What Buffon said is a big blasphemy : genius is not long-continued patience. Still, there is some truth in the statement, and more than people think, especially as regards our own day. Art! art! art! bitter deception! phantom that glows with light, only to lead one on to destruction.

Again—

I am growing so peevish about my writing. I am like a man whose ear is true but who plays falsely on the violin : his fingers refuse to reproduce precisely those sounds of which he has the inward sense. Then the tears come rolling down from the poor scraper's eyes and the bow falls from his hand.

Coming slowly or quickly, when it comes, as it came with so much labour of mind, but also with so much lustre, to Gustave Flaubert, this discovery of the word will be, like all artistic success and felicity, incapable of strict analysis : effect of an intuitive condition of mind, it must be recognised by like intuition on the part of the reader, and a sort of immediate sense. In every one of those masterly sentences of Flaubert there was, below all mere contrivance, shaping and afterthought, by some happy instantaneous concourse of the various faculties of the mind with each other, the exact apprehension of what was *needed* to carry the meaning. And that it fits with absolute justice will be a judgment of immediate sense in the appreciative reader. We all feel this in what may be called inspired translation. Well ! all language involves translation from inward to outward. In literature, as in all forms of art, there are the absolute and the merely relative or accessory beauties ; and precisely in that exact proportion of the term to its purpose is the absolute beauty of style, prose or verse. All the good qualities, the beauties, of verse also, are such, only as precise expression.

In the highest as in the lowliest literature, then, the one indispensable beauty is, after all, truth :—truth to bare fact in the latter, as to some personal sense of fact, diverted somewhat from men's ordinary sense of it, in the former ; truth there as accuracy, truth here as expression, that finest and most intimate form of truth, the *vraie vérité*. And what an eclectic principle this really is ! employing for its one sole purpose—that absolute accordance of expression to idea—all other literary beauties and excellences whatever : how many kinds of style it covers, explains, justifies, and at the same time safeguards ! Scott's facility, Flaubert's deeply pondered evocation of " the phrase," are equally good art. Say what you have to say, what you have a will to say, in the simplest, the most direct and exact manner possible, with no surplusage :—there, is the justification of the sentence so fortunately born, " entire, smooth, and round," that it needs no punctuation, and also (that is the point!) of the most elaborate period, if it be right in its elaboration. Here is the office of ornament : here also the purpose of restraint in ornament. As the exponent of truth, that austerity (the beauty, the function, of which in literature Flaubert understood so well) becomes not the correctness or purism of the mere scholar, but a security against the otiose, a jealous exclusion of what does not really tell towards the pursuit of relief, of life and vigour in the portraiture of one's sense. License again, the making free with rule, if it be indeed, as people fancy, a habit of genius, flinging aside or transforming all that opposes the liberty of beautiful production, will be but faith to one's own meaning. The seeming baldness of *Le Rouge et Le Noir* is nothing in itself ; the wild ornament of *Les Misérables* is nothing in itself ; and the restraint of Flaubert, amid a real natural opulence, only redoubled beauty—the phrase so large and so precise at the same time, hard as bronze, in service to the more perfect adaptation of words to their matter. Afterthoughts, retouchings, finish, will be of profit only so far as they too really serve to bring out the original, initiative, generative, sense in them.

In this way, according to the well-known saying, "The style is the man," complex or simple, in his individuality, his plenary sense of what he really has to say, his sense of the world ; all cautions regarding style arising out of so many natural scruples as to the medium through which alone he can expose that inward sense of things, the purity of this medium, its laws or tricks of refraction : nothing is to be left there which might give conveyance to any matter save that. Style in all its varieties, reserved or opulent, terse, abundant, musical, stimulant, academic, so long as each is really characteristic or expressive, finds thus its justification, the sumptuous good taste of Cicero being as truly the man himself, and not another, justified, yet insured inalienably to him, thereby, as would have been his portrait by Raffaelle, in full consular splendour, on his ivory chair.

A relegation, you may say perhaps—a relegation of style to the subjectivity, the mere caprice, of the individual, which must soon transform it into mannerism. Not so ! since there is, under the conditions supposed, for those elements of the man, for every lineament of the vision within, the one word, the one acceptable word, recognisable by the sensitive, by others "who have intelligence" in the matter, as absolutely as ever anything can be in the evanescent and delicate region of human language. The style, the manner, would be the man, not in his unreasoned and really uncharacteristic caprices, involuntary or affected, but in absolutely sincere apprehension of what is most real to him. But let us hear our French guide again.—

Styles (says Flaubert's commentator), *Styles*, as so many

peculiar moulds, each of which bears the mark of a particular writer, who is to pour into it the whole content of his ideas, were no part of his theory. What he believed in was *Style*: that is to say, a certain absolute and unique manner of expressing a thing, in all its intensity and colour. For him the *form* was the work itself. As in living creatures, the blood, nourishing the body, determines its very contour and external aspect, just so, to his mind, the *matter*, the basis, in a work of art, imposed, necessarily, the unique, the just expression, the measure, the rhythm—the *form* in all its characteristics.

If the style be the man, in all the colour and intensity of a veritable apprehension, it will be in a real sense " impersonal."

I said, thinking of books like Victor Hugo's *Les Misérables*, that prose literature was the characteristic art of the nineteenth century, as others, thinking of its triumphs since the youth of Bach, have assigned that place to music. Music and prose literature are, in one sense, the opposite terms of art ; the art of literature presenting to the imagination, through the intelligence, a range of interests, as free and various as those which music presents to it through sense. And certainly the tendency of what has been here said is to bring literature too under those conditions, by conformity to which music takes rank as the typically perfect art. If music be the ideal of all art whatever, precisely because in music it is impossible to distinguish the form from the substance or matter, the subject from the expression, then, literature, by finding its specific excellence in the absolute correspondence of the term to its import, will be but fulfilling the condition of all artistic quality in things everywhere, of all good art.

Good art, but not necessarily great art ; the distinction between great art and good art depending immediately, as regards literature at all events, not on its form, but on the matter. Thackeray's *Esmond*, surely, is greater art than *Vanity Fair*, by the greater dignity of its interests. It is on the quality of the matter it informs or controls, its compass, its variety, its alliance to great ends, or the depth of the note of revolt, or the largeness of hope in it, that the greatness of literary art depends, as *The Divine Comedy*, *Paradise Lost*, *Les Misérables*, *The English Bible*, are great art. Given the conditions I have tried to explain as constituting good art ;—then, if it be devoted further to the increase of men's happiness, to the redemption of the oppressed, or the enlargement of our sympathies with each other, or to such presentment of new or old truth about ourselves and our relation to the world as may ennoble and fortify us in our sojourn here, or immediately, as with Dante, to the glory of God, it will be also great art ; if, over and above those qualities I summed up as mind and soul—that colour and mystic perfume, and that reasonable structure, it has something of the soul of humanity in it, and finds its logical, its architectural place, in the great structure of human life.

1888.

WORDSWORTH

SOME English critics at the beginning of the present century had a great deal to say concerning a distinction, of much importance, as they thought, in the true estimate of poetry, between the *Fancy*, and another more powerful faculty—the *Imagination*. This metaphysical distinction, borrowed originally from the writings of German philosophers, and perhaps not always clearly apprehended by those who talked of it, involved a far deeper and more vital distinction, with which indeed all true criticism more or less directly has to do, the distinction, namely, between higher and lower degrees of intensity in the poet's perception of his subject, and in his concentration of himself upon his work. Of those who dwelt upon the metaphysical distinction between the Fancy and the Imagination, it was Wordsworth who made the most of it, assuming it as the basis for the final classification of his poetical writings ; and it is in these writings that the deeper and more vital distinction, which, as I have said, underlies the metaphysical

39

distinction, is most needed, and may best be illustrated.

For nowhere is there so perplexed a mixture as in Wordsworth's own poetry, of work touched with intense and individual power, with work of almost no character at all. He has much conventional sentiment, and some of that insincere poetic diction, against which his most serious critical efforts were directed : the reaction in his political ideas, consequent on the excesses of 1795, makes him, at times, a mere declaimer on moral and social topics ; and he seems, sometimes, to force an unwilling pen, and write by rule. By making the most of these blemishes it is possible to obscure the true æsthetic value of his work, just as his life also, a life of much quiet delicacy and independence, might easily be placed in a false focus, and made to appear a somewhat tame theme in illustration of the more obvious parochial virtues. And those who wish to understand his influence, and experience his peculiar savour, must bear with patience the presence of an alien element in Wordsworth's work, which never coalesced with what is really delightful in it, nor underwent his special power. Who that values his writings most has not felt the intrusion there, from time to time, of something tedious and prosaic ?   Of all poets equally great, he would gain most by a skilfully made anthology. Such a selection would show, in truth, not so much what he was, or to himself or others

seemed to be, as what, by the more energetic
and fertile quality in his writings, he was ever
tending to become. And the mixture in his
work, as it actually stands, is so perplexed, that
one fears to miss the least promising composition
even, lest some precious morsel should be lying
hidden within—the few perfect lines, the phrase,
the single word perhaps, to which he often works
up mechanically through a poem, almost the
whole of which may be tame enough. He who
thought that in all creative work the larger part
was *given* passively, to the recipient mind, who
waited so dutifully upon the gift, to whom so
large a measure was sometimes given, had his
times also of desertion and relapse ; and he has
permitted the impress of these too to remain in
his work. And this duality there—the fitfulness
with which the higher qualities manifest themselves in it, gives the effect in his poetry of a
power not altogether his own, or under his
control, which comes and goes when it will, lifting or lowering a matter, poor in itself ; so that
that old fancy which made the poet's art an
enthusiasm, a form of divine possession, seems
almost literally true of him.

This constant suggestion of an absolute duality
between higher and lower moods, and the work
done in them, stimulating one always to look
below the surface, makes the reading of Wordsworth an excellent sort of training towards the
things of art and poetry. It begets in those,

APPRECIATIONS

who, coming across him in youth, can bear him
at all, a habit of reading between the lines, a
faith in the effect of concentration and collected-
ness of mind in the right appreciation of poetry,
an expectation of things, in this order, coming
to one by means of a right discipline of the
temper as well as of the intellect. He meets us
with the promise that he has much, and something very peculiar, to give us, if we will follow
a certain difficult way, and seems to have the
secret of a special and privileged state of mind.
And those who have undergone his influence, and followed this difficult way, are like
people who have passed through some initiation, a *disciplina arcani*, by submitting to
which they become able constantly to distinguish in art, speech, feeling, manners, that
which is organic, animated, expressive, from
that which is only conventional, derivative,
inexpressive.

But although the necessity of selecting these
precious morsels for oneself is an opportunity for
the exercise of Wordsworth's peculiar influence,
and induces a kind of just criticism and true
estimate of it, yet the purely literary product
would have been more excellent, had the writer
himself purged away that alien element. How
perfect would have been the little treasury, shut
between the covers of how thin a book! Let
us suppose the desired separation made, the
electric thread untwined, the golden pieces,

great and small, lying apart together.[1]   What
are the peculiarities of this residue ?   What
special sense does Wordsworth exercise, and
what instincts does he satisfy ?   What are the
subjects and the motives which in him excite
the imaginative faculty ?   What are the qualities
in things and persons which he values, the impression and sense of which he can convey to
others, in an extraordinary way ?

An intimate consciousness of the expression
of natural things, which weighs, listens, pene-
trates, where the earlier mind passed roughly by,
is a large element in the complexion of modern
poetry.   It has been remarked as a fact in
mental history again and again.   It reveals itself
in many forms ; but is strongest and most attractive in what is strongest and most attractive in
modern literature.   It is exemplified, almost
equally, by writers as unlike each other as
Senancour and Théophile Gautier : as a singular
chapter in the history of the human mind, its
growth might be traced from Rousseau to
Chateaubriand, from Chateaubriand to Victor
Hugo : it has doubtless some latent connexion
with those pantheistic theories which locate an
intelligent soul in material things, and have
largely exercised men's minds in some modern
systems of philosophy : it is traceable even in

[1] Since this essay was written, such selections have been made,
with excellent taste, by Matthew Arnold and Professor Knight.

the graver writings of historians : it makes as much difference between ancient and modern landscape art, as there is between the rough masks of an early mosaic and a portrait by Reynolds or Gainsborough. Of this new sense, the writings of Wordsworth are the central and elementary expression : he is more simply and entirely occupied with it than any other poet, though there are fine expressions of precisely the same thing in so different a poet as Shelley. There was in his own character a certain contentment, a sort of inborn religious placidity, seldom found united with a sensibility so mobile as his, which was favourable to the quiet, habitual observation of inanimate, or imperfectly animate, existence. His life of eighty years is divided by no very profoundly felt incidents : its changes are almost wholly inward, and it falls into broad, untroubled, perhaps somewhat monotonous spaces. What it most resembles is the life of one of those early Italian or Flemish painters, who, just because their minds were full of heavenly visions, passed, some of them, the better part of sixty years in quiet, systematic industry. This placid life matured a quite unusual sensibility, really innate in him, to the sights and sounds of the natural world—the flower and its shadow on the stone, the cuckoo and its echo. The poem of *Resolution and Independence* is a storehouse of such records : for its fulness of imagery it may be compared to Keats's *Saint Agnes' Eve*. To

read one of his longer pastoral poems for the
first time, is like a day spent in a new country :
the memory is crowded for a while with its
precise and vivid incidents—

> The pliant harebell swinging in the breeze
> On some grey rock ;—
>
> The single sheep and the one blasted tree
> And the bleak music from that old stone wall ;—
>
> In the meadows and the lower ground
> Was all the sweetness of a common dawn ;—
>
> And that green corn all day is rustling in thine ears.

Clear and delicate at once, as he is in the
outlining of visible imagery, he is more clear
and delicate still, and finely scrupulous, in the
noting of sounds ; so that he conceives of noble
sound as even moulding the human countenance
to nobler types, and as something actually " pro-
faned " by colour, by visible form, or image.
He has a power likewise of realising, and con-
veying to the consciousness of the reader, abstract
and elementary impressions—silence, darkness,
absolute motionlessness : or, again, the whole
complex sentiment of a particular place, the
abstract expression of desolation in the long
white road, of peacefulness in a particular fold-
ing of the hills. In the airy building of the
brain, a special day or hour even, comes to have
for him a sort of personal identity, a spirit or
angel given to it, by which, for its exceptional

insight, or the happy light upon it, it has a presence in one's history, and acts there, as a separate power or accomplishment ; and he has celebrated in many of his poems the " efficacious spirit," which, as he says, resides in these " particular spots " of time.

It is to such a world, and to a world of congruous meditation thereon, that we see him retiring in his but lately published poem of *The Recluse*—taking leave, without much count of costs, of the world of business, of action and ambition, as also of all that for the majority of mankind counts as sensuous enjoyment.[1]

And so it came about that this sense of a life in natural objects, which in most poetry is but a rhetorical artifice, is with Wordsworth the assertion of what for him is almost literal fact. To him every natural object seemed to possess more or less of a moral or spiritual life, to be

---

[1] In Wordsworth's prefatory advertisement to the first edition of *The Prelude*, published in 1850, it is stated that that work was intended to be introductory to *The Recluse ;* and that *The Recluse*, if completed, would have consisted of three parts. The second part is " The Excursion." The third part was only planned ; but the first book of the first part was left in manuscript by Wordsworth —though in manuscript, it is said, in no great condition of forwardness for the printers. This book, now for the first time printed *in extenso* (a very noble passage from it found place in that prose advertisement to *The Excursion*), is included in the latest edition of Wordsworth by Mr. John Morley. It was well worth adding to the poet's great bequest to English literature. A true student of his work, who has formulated for himself what he supposes to be the leading characteristics of Wordsworth's genius, will feel, we think, lively interest in testing them by the various fine passages in

capable of a companionship with man, full of expression, of inexplicable affinities and delicacies of intercourse. An emanation, a particular spirit, belonged, not to the moving leaves or water only, but to the distant peak of the hills arising suddenly, by some change of perspective, above the nearer horizon, to the passing space of light across the plain, to the lichened Druidic stone even, for a certain weird fellowship in it with the moods of men. It was like a "survival," in the peculiar intellectual temperament of a man of letters at the end of the eighteenth century, of that primitive condition, which some philosophers have traced in the general history of human culture, wherein all outward objects

what is here presented for the first time. Let the following serve for a sample :—

> Thickets full of songsters, and the voice
> Of lordly birds, an unexpected sound
> Heard now and then from morn to latest eve,
> Admonishing the man who walks below
> Of solitude and silence in the sky :—
> These have we, and a thousand nooks of earth
> Have also these, but nowhere else is found,
> Nowhere (or is it fancy?) can be found
> The one sensation that is here ; 'tis here,
> Here as it found its way into my heart
> In childhood, here as it abides by day,
> By night, here only ; or in chosen minds
> That take it with them hence, where'er they go.
> —'Tis, but I cannot name it, 'tis the sense
> Of majesty, and beauty, and repose,
> A blended holiness of earth and sky,
> Something that makes this individual spot,
> This small abiding-place of many men,
> A termination, and a last retreat,
> A centre, come from wheresoe'er you will,
> A whole without dependence or defect,
> Made for itself, and happy in itself,
> Perfect contentment, Unity entire.

alike, including even the works of men's hands, were believed to be endowed with animation, and the world was "full of souls"—that mood in which the old Greek gods were first begotten, and which had many strange aftergrowths. In the early ages, this belief, delightful as its effects on poetry often are, was but the result of a crude intelligence. But, in Wordsworth, such power of seeing life, such perception of a soul, in inanimate things, came of an exceptional susceptibility to the impressions of eye and ear, and was, in its essence, a kind of sensuousness. At least, it is only in a temperament exceptionally susceptible on the sensuous side, that this sense of the expressiveness of outward things comes to be so large a part of life. That he awakened "a sort of thought in sense," is Shelley's just estimate of this element in Wordsworth's poetry.

And it was through nature, thus ennobled by a semblance of passion and thought, that he approached the spectacle of human life. Human life, indeed, is for him, at first, only an additional, accidental grace on an expressive landscape. When he thought of man, it was of man as in the presence and under the influence of these effective natural objects, and linked to them by many associations. The close connexion of man with natural objects, the habitual association of his thoughts and feelings with a particular spot of earth, has sometimes seemed to

48

degrade those who are subject to its influence, as if it did but reinforce that physical connexion of our nature with the actual lime and clay of the soil, which is always drawing us nearer to our end. But for Wordsworth, these influences tended to the dignity of human nature, because they tended to tranquillise it. By raising nature to the level of human thought he gives it power and expression : he subdues man to the level of nature, and gives him thereby a certain breadth and coolness and solemnity. The leech-gatherer on the moor, the woman " stepping westward," are for him natural objects, almost in the same sense as the aged thorn, or the lichened rock on the heath. In this sense the leader of the " Lake School," in spite of an earnest preoccupation with man, his thoughts, his destiny, is the poet of nature. And of nature, after all, in its modesty. The English lake country has, of course, its grandeurs. But the peculiar function of Wordsworth's genius, as carrying in it a power to open out the soul of apparently little or familiar things, would have found its true test had he become the poet of Surrey, say ! and the prophet of its life. The glories of Italy and Switzerland, though he did write a little about them, had too potent a material life of their own to serve greatly his poetic purpose.

Religious sentiment, consecrating the affections and natural regrets of the human heart, above all, that pitiful awe and care for the perishing human clay, of which relic-worship is but the corruption, has always had much to do with localities, with the thoughts which attach themselves to actual scenes and places. Now what is true of it everywhere, is truest of it in those secluded valleys where one generation after another maintains the same abiding-place ; and it was on this side, that Wordsworth apprehended religion most strongly. Consisting, as it did so much, in the recognition of local sanctities, in the habit of connecting the stones and trees of a particular spot of earth with the great events of life, till the low walls, the green mounds, the half-obliterated epitaphs seemed full of voices, and a sort of natural oracles, the very religion of these people of the dales appeared but as another link between them and the earth, and was literally a religion of nature. It tranquillised them by bringing them under the placid rule of traditional and narrowly localised observances. " Grave livers," they seemed to him, under this aspect, with stately speech, and something of that natural dignity of manners, which underlies the highest courtesy.

And, seeing man thus as a part of nature, elevated and solemnised in proportion as his daily life and occupations brought him into companionship with permanent natural objects, his very religion forming new links for him with the narrow limits of the valley, the low vaults of his church, the rough stones of his home, made intense for him now with profound sentiment, Wordsworth was able to appreciate passion in the lowly. He chooses to depict people from humble life, because, being nearer to nature than others, they are on the whole more impassioned, certainly more direct in their expression of passion, than other men : it is for this direct expression of passion, that he values their humble words. In much that he said in exaltation of rural life, he was but pleading indirectly for that sincerity, that perfect fidelity to one's own inward presentations, to the precise features of the picture within, without which any profound poetry is impossible. It was not for their tameness, but for this passionate sincerity, that he chose incidents and situations from common life, "related in a selection of language really used by men." He constantly endeavours to bring his language near to the real language of men : to the real language of men, however, not on the dead level of their ordinary intercourse, but in select moments of vivid sensation, when this language is winnowed and ennobled by excitement. There are poets who have chosen rural life as their subject, for the sake of its passionless repose, and times when Wordsworth himself extols the mere calm and dispassionate survey of things as the highest aim of poetical culture. But it was not for such passionless calm that he preferred the scenes of pastoral life ; and the meditative poet, sheltering

APPRECIATIONS

himself, as it might seem, from the agitations of
the outward world, is in reality only clearing the
scene for the great exhibitions of emotion, and
what he values most is the almost elementary
expression of elementary feelings.

And so he has much for those who value
highly the concentrated presentment of passion,
who appraise men and women by their susceptibility to it, and art and poetry as they afford the
spectacle of it.   Breaking from time to time into
the pensive spectacle of their daily toil, their
occupations near to nature, come those great
elementary feelings, lifting and solemnising their
language and giving it a natural music.   The
great, distinguishing passion came to Michael
by the sheepfold, to Ruth by the wayside, adding
these humble children of the furrow to the true
aristocracy of passionate souls.   In this respect,
Wordsworth's work resembles most that of
George Sand, in those of her novels which
depict country life.   With a penetrative pathos,
which puts him in the same rank with the
masters of the sentiment of pity in literature,
with Meinhold and Victor Hugo, he collects
all the traces of vivid excitement which were to
be found in that pastoral world—the girl who
rung her father's knell; the unborn infant feeling
about its mother's heart; the instinctive touches
of children; the sorrows of the wild creatures,
even—their home-sickness, their strange yearn-
ings; the tales of passionate regret that hang

by a ruined farm-building, a heap of stones, a
deserted sheepfold ; that gay, false, adventurous,
outer world, which breaks in from time to time
to bewilder and deflower these quiet homes ; not
" passionate sorrow " only, for the overthrow
of the soul's beauty, but the loss of, or careless-
ness for personal beauty even, in those whom
men have wronged—their pathetic wanness ; the
sailor " who, in his heart, was half a shepherd
on the stormy seas " ; the wild woman teaching
her child to pray for her betrayer ; incidents like
the making of the shepherd's staff, or that of the
young boy laying the first stone of the sheepfold ;
—all the pathetic episodes of their humble
existence, their longing, their wonder at fortune,
their poor pathetic pleasures, like the pleasures
of children, won so hardly in the struggle for
bare existence ; their yearning towards each
other, in their darkened houses, or at their early
toil. A sort of biblical depth and solemnity
hangs over this strange, new, passionate, pastoral
world, of which he first raised the image, and
the reflection of which some of our best modern
fiction has caught from him.

He pondered much over the philosophy of
his poetry, and reading deeply in the history of
his own mind, seems at times to have passed the
borders of a world of strange speculations, incon-
sistent enough, had he cared to note such incon-
sistencies, with those traditional beliefs, which

were otherwise the object of his devout acceptance. Thinking of the high value he set upon
customariness, upon all that is habitual, local,
rooted in the ground, in matters of religious
sentiment, you might sometimes regard him as
one tethered down to a world, refined and peaceful indeed, but with no broad outlook, a world
protected, but somewhat narrowed, by the influence of received ideas. But he is at times also
something very different from this, and something
much bolder. A chance expression is overheard
and placed in a new connexion, the sudden
memory of a thing long past occurs to him, a
distant object is relieved for a while by a random
gleam of light — accidents turning up for a
moment what lies below the surface of our
immediate experience—and he passes from the
humble graves and lowly arches of " the little
rock-like pile " of a Westmoreland church, on
bold trains of speculative thought, and comes,
from point to point, into strange contact with
thoughts which have visited, from time to time,
far more venturesome, perhaps errant, spirits.

He had pondered deeply, for instance, on those
strange reminiscences and forebodings, which
seem to make our lives stretch before and behind
us, beyond where we can see or touch anything,
or trace the lines of connexion. Following the
soul, backwards and forwards, on these endless
ways, his sense of man's dim, potential powers
became a pledge to him, indeed, of a future life,

but carried him back also to that mysterious notion of an earlier state of existence—the fancy of the Platonists—the old heresy of Origen. It was in this mood that he conceived those oft-reiterated regrets for a half-ideal childhood, when the relics of Paradise still clung about the soul—a childhood, as it seemed, full of the fruits of old age, lost for all, in a degree, in the passing away of the youth of the world, lost for each one, over again, in the passing away of actual youth. It is this ideal childhood which he celebrates in his famous *Ode on the Recollections of Childhood*, and some other poems which may be grouped around it, such as the lines on *Tintern Abbey*, and something like what he describes was actually truer of himself than he seems to have understood ; for his own most delightful poems were really the instinctive productions of earlier life, and most surely for him, " the first diviner influence of this world " passed away, more and more completely, in his contact with experience.

Sometimes as he dwelt upon those moments of profound, imaginative power, in which the outward object appears to take colour and ex-pression, a new nature almost, from the prompting of the observant mind, the actual world would, as it were, dissolve and detach itself, flake by flake, and he himself seemed to be the creator, and when he would the destroyer, of the world in which he lived—that old isolating thought of many a brain-sick mystic of ancient and modern times.

APPRECIATIONS

At other times, again, in those periods of intense susceptibility, in which he appeared to himself as but the passive recipient of external influences, he was attracted by the thought of a spirit of life in outward things, a single, all-pervading mind in them, of which man, and even the poet's imaginative energy, are but moments—that old dream of the *anima mundi*, the mother of all things and their grave, in which some had desired to lose themselves, and others had become indifferent to the distinctions of good and evil. It would come, sometimes, like the sign of the *macrocosm* to Faust in his cell : the network of man and nature was seen to be pervaded by a common, universal life : a new, bold thought lifted him above the furrow, above the green turf of the Westmoreland church-yard, to a world altogether different in its vagueness and vastness, and the narrow glen was full of the brooding power of one universal spirit.

And so he has something, also, for those who feel the fascination of bold speculative ideas, who are really capable of rising upon them to conditions of poetical thought. He uses them, indeed, always with a very fine apprehension of the limits within which alone philosophical imaginings have any place in true poetry ; and using them only for poetical purposes, is not too careful even to make them consistent with each other. To him, theories which for other men bring a world of technical diction, brought perfect form and expression, as in those two lofty books of *The Prelude*, which describe the decay and the restoration of Imagination and Taste. Skirting the borders of this world of bewildering heights and depths, he got but the first exciting influence of it, that joyful enthusiasm which great imaginative theories prompt, when the mind first comes to have an understanding of them ; and it is not under the influence of these thoughts that his poetry becomes tedious or loses its blitheness. He keeps them, too, always within certain ethical bounds, so that no word of his could offend the simplest of those simple souls which are always the largest portion of mankind. But it is, nevertheless, the contact of these thoughts, the speculative boldness in them, which constitutes, at least for some minds, the secret attraction of much of his best poetry —the sudden passage from lowly thoughts and places to the majestic forms of philosophical imagination, the play of these forms over a world so different, enlarging so strangely the bounds of its humble churchyards, and breaking such a wild light on the graves of christened children.

And these moods always brought with them faultless expression. In regard to expression, as with feeling and thought, the duality of the higher and lower moods was absolute. It belonged to the higher, the imaginative mood, and was the pledge of its reality, to bring the appropriate language with it. In him, when the really poetical motive worked at all, it united, with absolute justice, the word and the idea ; each, in the imaginative flame, becoming inseparably one with the other, by that fusion of matter and form, which is the characteristic of the highest poetical expression. His words are themselves thought and feeling ; not eloquent, or musical words merely, but that sort of creative language which carries the reality of what it depicts, directly, to the consciousness.

The music of mere metre performs but a limited, yet a very peculiar and subtly ascertained function, in Wordsworth's poetry. With him, metre is but an additional grace, accessory to that deeper music of words and sounds, that moving power, which they exercise in the nobler prose no less than in formal poetry. It is a sedative to that excitement, an excitement sometimes almost painful, under which the language, alike of poetry and prose, attains a rhythmical power, independent of metrical combination, and dependent rather on some subtle adjustment of the elementary sounds of words themselves to the image or feeling they convey. Yet some of his pieces, pieces prompted by a sort of half-playful mysticism, like the *Daffodils* and *The Two April Mornings*, are distinguished by a certain quaint gaiety of metre, and rival by their perfect execution, in this respect, similar pieces among our own Elizabethan, or contemporary French poetry.

WORDSWORTH

And those who take up these poems after an interval of months, or years perhaps, may be surprised at finding how well old favourites wear, how their strange, inventive turns of diction or thought still send through them the old feeling of surprise. Those who lived about Wordsworth were all great lovers of the older English literature, and oftentimes there came out in him a noticeable likeness to our earlier poets. He quotes unconsciously, but with new power of meaning, a clause from one of Shakespeare's sonnets ; and, as with some other men's most famous work, the *Ode on the Recollections of Childhood* had its anticipator.[1] He drew something too from the unconscious mysticism of the old English language itself, drawing out the inward significance of its racy idiom, and the not wholly unconscious poetry of the language used by the simplest people under strong excitement—language, therefore, at its origin.

The office of the poet is not that of the moralist, and the first aim of Wordsworth's poetry is to give the reader a peculiar kind of pleasure. But through his poetry, and through this pleasure in it, he does actually convey to the reader an extraordinary wisdom in the things of practice. One lesson, if men must have lessons, he conveys more clearly than all, the supreme importance of contemplation in the conduct of life.

[1] Henry Vaughan, in *The Retreat*.

Contemplation—impassioned contemplation—that, is with Wordsworth the end-in-itself, the perfect end. We see the majority of mankind going most often to definite ends, lower or higher ends, as their own instincts may determine ; but the end may never be attained, and the means not be quite the right means, great ends and little ones alike being, for the most part, distant, and the ways to them, in this dim world, somewhat vague. Meantime, to higher or lower ends, they move too often with something of a sad countenance, with hurried and ignoble gait, becoming, unconsciously, something like thorns, in their anxiety to bear grapes ; it being possible for people, in the pursuit of even great ends, to become themselves thin and impoverished in spirit and temper, thus diminishing the sum of perfection in the world, at its very sources. We understand this when it is a question of mean, or of intensely selfish ends—of Grandet, or Javert. We think it bad morality to say that the end justifies the means, and we know how false to all higher conceptions of the religious life is the type of one who is ready to do evil that good may come. We contrast with such dark, mistaken eagerness, a type like that of Saint Catherine of Siena, who made the means to her ends so attractive, that she has won for herself an undying place in the *House Beautiful*, not by her rectitude of soul only, but by its " fairness "—by those quite different qualities

which commend themselves to the poet and
the artist.

Yet, for most of us, the conception of means
and ends covers the whole of life, and is the
exclusive type or figure under which we represent
our lives to ourselves. Such a figure, reducing
all things to machinery, though it has on its side
the authority of that old Greek moralist who has
fixed for succeeding generations the outline of
the theory of right living, is too like a mere
picture or description of men's lives as we
actually find them, to be the basis of the higher
ethics. It covers the meanness of men's daily
lives, and much of the dexterity and the vigour
with which they pursue what may seem to
them the good of themselves or of others ; but
not the intangible perfection of those whose
ideal is rather in *being* than in *doing*—not those
manners which are, in the deepest as in the
simplest sense, *morals*, and without which one
cannot so much as offer a cup of water to a poor
man without offence—not the part of " antique
Rachel," sitting in the company of Beatrice ;
and even the moralist might well endeavour
rather to withdraw men from the too exclusive
consideration of means and ends, in life.

Against this predominance of machinery in
our existence, Wordsworth's poetry, like all great
art and poetry, is a continual protest. Justify
rather the end by the means, it seems to say :
whatever may become of the fruit, make sure of

the flowers and the leaves. It was justly said,
therefore, by one who had meditated very profoundly on the true relation of means to ends in
life, and on the distinction between what is
desirable in itself and what is desirable only as
machinery, that when the battle which he and
his friends were waging had been won, the
world would need more than ever those qualities which Wordsworth was keeping alive and
nourishing.[1]

That the end of life is not action but contemplation—*being* as distinct from *doing*—a certain
disposition of the mind : is, in some shape or
other, the principle of all the higher morality.
In poetry, in art, if you enter into their true
spirit at all, you touch this principle, in a
measure : these, by their very sterility, are a
type of beholding for the mere joy of beholding.
To treat life in the spirit of art, is to make life a
thing in which means and ends are identified :
to encourage such treatment, the true moral
significance of art and poetry. Wordsworth,
and other poets who have been like him in
ancient or more recent times, are the masters,
the experts, in this art of impassioned contemplation. Their work is, not to teach lessons, or
enforce rules, or even to stimulate us to noble
ends ; but to withdraw the thoughts for a little
while from the mere machinery of life, to fix

[1] See an interesting paper, by Mr. John Morley, on " The
Death of Mr. Mill," *Fortnightly Review*, June 1873.

them, with appropriate emotions, on the spectacle of those great facts in man's existence which no machinery affects, " on the great and universal passions of men, the most general and interesting of their occupations, and the entire world of nature,"—on " the operations of the elements and the appearances of the visible universe, on storm and sunshine, on the revolutions of the seasons, on cold and heat, on loss of friends and kindred, on injuries and resentments, on gratitude and hope, on fear and sorrow." To witness this spectacle with appropriate emotions is the aim of all culture ; and of these emotions poetry like Wordsworth's is a great nourisher and stimulant. He sees nature full of sentiment and excitement ; he sees men and women as parts of nature, passionate, excited, in strange grouping and con-nexion with the grandeur and beauty of the natural world :—images, in his own words, " of man suffering, amid awful forms and powers."

Such is the figure of the more powerful and original poet, hidden away, in part, under those weaker elements in Wordsworth's poetry, which for some minds determine their entire character ; a poet somewhat bolder and more passionate than might at first sight be supposed, but not too bold for true poetical taste ; an unimpassioned writer, you might sometimes fancy, yet thinking the chief aim, in life and art alike, to be a certain deep emotion ; seeking most often the great

elementary passions in lowly places ; having at
least this condition of all impassioned work, that
he aims always at an absolute sincerity of feeling
and diction, so that he is the true forerunner of
the deepest and most passionate poetry of our
own day ; yet going back also, with something
of a protest against the conventional fervour oí
much of the poetry popular in his own time,
to those older English poets, whose unconscious
likeness often comes out in him.

1874.

COLERIDGE[1]

Forms of intellectual and spiritual culture sometimes exercise their subtlest and most artful
charm when life is already passing from them.
Searching and irresistible as are the changes of
the human spirit on its way to perfection, there
is yet so much elasticity of temper that what
must pass away sooner or later is not disengaged
all at once, even from the highest order of minds.
Nature, which by one law of development
evolves ideas, hypotheses, modes of inward life,
and represses them in turn, has in this way provided that the earlier growth should propel its
fibres into the later, and so transmit the whole
of its forces in an unbroken continuity of life.
Then comes the spectacle of the reserve of the
elder generation exquisitely refined by the antagonism of the new. That current of new life
chastens them while they contend against it.
Weaker minds fail to perceive the change : the
clearest minds abandon themselves to it. To

[1] The latter part of this paper, like that on Dante Gabriel
Rossetti, was contributed to Mr. T. H. Ward's *English Poets.*

feel the change everywhere, yet not abandon oneself to it, is a situation of difficulty and contention. Communicating, in this way, to the passing stage of culture, the charm of what is chastened, high-strung, athletic, they yet detach the highest minds from the past, by pressing home its difficulties and finally proving it impossible. Such has been the charm of many leaders of lost causes in philosophy and in religion. It is the special charm of Coleridge, in connexion with those older methods of philosophic inquiry, over which the empirical philosophy of our day has triumphed.

Modern thought is distinguished from ancient by its cultivation of the "relative" spirit in place of the "absolute." Ancient philosophy sought to arrest every object in an eternal outline, to fix thought in a necessary formula, and the varieties of life in a classification by "kinds," or *genera*. To the modern spirit nothing is, or can be rightly known, except relatively and under conditions. The philosophical conception of the relative has been developed in modern times through the influence of the sciences of observation. Those sciences reveal types of life evanescing into each other by inexpressible refinements of change. Things pass into their opposites by accumulation of undefinable quantities. The growth of those sciences consists in a continual analysis of facts of rough and general observation into groups of facts more precise and minute.

COLERIDGE

The faculty for truth is recognised as a power of distinguishing and fixing delicate and fugitive detail. The moral world is ever in contact with the physical, and the relative spirit has invaded moral philosophy from the ground of the inductive sciences. There it has started a new analysis of the relations of body and mind, good and evil, freedom and necessity. Hard and abstract moralities are yielding to a more exact estimate of the subtlety and complexity of our life. Always, as an organism increases in perfection, the conditions of its life become more complex. Man is the most complex of the products of nature. Character merges into temperament : the nervous system refines itself into intellect. Man's physical organism is played upon not only by the physical conditions about it, but by remote laws of inheritance, the vibration of long-past acts reaching him in the midst of the new order of things in which he lives. When we have estimated these conditions he is still not yet simple and isolated ; for the mind of the race, the character of the age, sway him this way or that through the medium of language and current ideas. It seems as if the most opposite statements about him were alike true : he is so receptive, all the influences of nature and of society ceaselessly playing upon him, so that every hour in, his life is unique, changed altogether by a stray word, or glance, or touch. It is the truth of these relations that experience

gives us, not the truth of eternal outlines
ascertained once for all, but a world of fine
gradations and subtly linked conditions, shifting
intricately as we ourselves change—and bids us,
by a constant clearing of the organs of observation and perfecting of analysis, to make what we
can of these. To the intellect, the critical spirit,
just these subtleties of effect are more precious
than anything else. What is lost in precision of
form is gained in intricacy of expression. It is
no vague scholastic abstraction that will satisfy
the speculative instinct in our modern minds.
Who would change the colour or curve of a rose-
leaf for that οὐσία ἀχρώματος, ἀσχημάτιστος, ἀναφὴς—
that colourless, formless, intangible, being—Plato
put so high ? For the true illustration of the
speculative temper is not the Hindoo mystic, lost
to sense, understanding, individuality, but one
such as Goethe, to whom every moment of
life brought its contribution of experimental,
individual knowledge ; by whom no touch of
the world of form, colour, and passion was
disregarded.

Now the literary life of Coleridge was a
disinterested struggle against the relative spirit.
With a strong native bent towards the tracking
of all questions, critical or practical, to first
principles, he is ever restlessly scheming to
" apprehend the absolute," to affirm it effectively,
to get it acknowledged. It was an effort, surely,
an effort of sickly thought, that saddened his

mind, and limited the operation of his unique
poetic gift.

So what the reader of our own generation will
least find in Coleridge's prose writings is the
excitement of the literary sense. And yet, in
those grey volumes, we have the larger part of
the production of one who made way ever by a
charm, the charm of voice, of aspect, of language,
above all by the intellectual charm of new,
moving, luminous ideas. Perhaps the chief
offence in Coleridge is an excess of seriousness, a
seriousness arising not from any moral principle,
but from a misconception of the perfect manner.
There is a certain shade of unconcern, the perfect
manner of the eighteenth century, which may
be thought to mark complete culture in the
handling of abstract questions. The humanist,
the possessor of that complete culture, does not
" weep " over the failure of " a theory of the
quantification of the predicate," nor " shriek "
over the fall of a philosophical formula. A kind
of humour is, in truth, one of the conditions of
the just mental attitude, in the criticism of by-
past stages of thought. Humanity cannot afford
to be too serious about them, any more than a
man of good sense can afford to be too serious in
looking back upon his own childhood. Plato,
whom Coleridge claims as the first of his spiritual
ancestors, Plato, as we remember him, a true
humanist, holds his theories lightly, glances with
a somewhat blithe and naive inconsequence from

one view to another, not anticipating the burden
of importance " views " will one day have for
men. In reading him one feels how lately it
was that Crœsus thought it a paradox to say that
external prosperity was not necessarily happiness.
But on Coleridge lies the whole weight of the
sad reflection that has since come into the world,
with which for us the air is full, which the
" children in the market-place " repeat to each
other. His very language is forced and broken
lest some saving formula should be lost—*distinc-
tities, enucleation, pentad of operative Christianity*;
he has a whole armoury of these terms, and
expects to turn the tide of human thought by
fixing the sense of such expressions as " reason,"
" understanding," " idea." Again, he lacks the
jealousy of a true artist in excluding all associations that have no colour, or charm, or gladness
in them ; and everywhere allows the impress of
a somewhat inferior theological literature.

" I was driven from life in motion to life in
thought and sensation : " so Coleridge sums up
his childhood, with its delicacy, its sensitiveness,
and passion. But at twenty-five he was exercis-
ing a wonderful charm, and had already defined
for himself his peculiar line of intellectual
activity. He had an odd, attractive gift of
conversation, or rather of monologue, as Madame
de Staël observed of him, full of *bizarreries*, with
the rapid alternations of a dream, and here or
there an unexpected summons into a world

strange to the hearer, abounding in images drawn from a sort of divided imperfect life, the consciousness of the opium-eater, as of one to whom the external world penetrated only in part, and, blent with all this, passages of deep obscurity, precious, if at all, only for their musical cadence, echoes in Coleridge of the eloquence of those older English writers of whom he was so ardent a lover. And all through this brilliant early manhood we may discern the power of the "Asiatic" temperament, of that voluptuousness, which is connected perhaps with his appreciation of the intimacy, the almost mystical communion of touch, between nature and man. "I am much better," he writes, "and my new and tender health is all over me like a voluptuous feeling." And whatever fame, or charm, or life-inspiring gift he has had as a speculative thinker, is the vibration of the interest he excited then, the propulsion into years which clouded his early promise of that first buoyant, irresistible, self-assertion. So great is even the indirect power of a sincere effort towards the ideal life, of even a temporary escape of the spirit from routine.

In 1798 he visited Germany, then, the only half-known, "promised land," of the metaphysical, the "absolute," philosophy. A beautiful fragment of this period remains, describing a spring excursion to the Brocken. His excitement still vibrates in it. Love, all joyful states of mind, are self-expressive : they loosen the tongue, they fill the thoughts with sensuous images, they harmonise one with the world of sight. We hear of the " rich graciousness and courtesy " of Coleridge's manner, of the white and delicate skin, the abundant black hair, the full, almost animal lips—that whole physiognomy of the dreamer, already touched with narcotism. One says, of the beginning of one of his Unitarian sermons : " His voice rose like a stream of rich, distilled perfumes ; " another, " He talks like an angel, and does—nothing ! "

The *Aids to Reflection*, *The Friend*, *The Biographia Literaria* : those books came from one whose vocation was in the world of the imagination, the theory and practice of poetry. And yet, perhaps, of all books that have been influential in modern times, they are furthest from artistic form—bundles of notes ; the original matter inseparably mixed up with that borrowed from others ; the whole, just that mere preparation for an artistic effect which the finished literary artist would be careful one day to destroy. Here, again, we have a trait profoundly characteristic of Coleridge. He sometimes attempts to reduce a phase of thought, subtle and exquisite, to conditions too rough for it. He uses a purely speculative gift for direct moral edification. Scientific truth is a thing fugitive, relative, full of fine gradations : he tries to fix it in absolute formulas. The *Aids to Reflection*, *The Friend*, are efforts to propagate the volatile spirit of conversation into the less ethereal fabric of a written book ; and it is only here or there that the poorer matter becomes vibrant, is really lifted by the spirit.

De Quincey said of him that " he wanted better bread than can be made with wheat : " Lamb, that from childhood he had " hungered for eternity." Yet the faintness, the continuous dissolution, whatever its cause, which soon supplanted the buoyancy of his first wonderful years, had its own consumptive refinements, and even brought, as to the " Beautiful Soul " in *Wilhelm Meister*, a faint religious ecstasy—that " singing in the sails " which is not of the breeze. Here again is one of his occasional notes :—

" In looking at objects of nature while I am thinking, as at yonder moon, dim-glimmering through the window-pane, I seem rather to be seeking, as it were asking, a symbolical language for something within me, that already and for ever exists, than observing anything new. Even when the latter is the case, yet still I have always an obscure feeling, as if that new phenomenon were the dim awaking of a forgotten or hidden truth of my inner nature. While I was preparing the pen to make this remark, I lost the train of thought which had led me to it."

What a distemper of the eye of the mind ! What an almost bodily distemper there is in that ! Coleridge's intellectual sorrows were many ;

but he had one singular intellectual happiness.
With an inborn taste for transcendental philosophy, he lived just at the time when that philosophy took an immense spring in Germany, and
connected itself with an impressive literary movement. He had the good luck to light upon it
in its freshness, and introduce it to his country-
men. What an opportunity for one reared on
the colourless analytic English philosophies of
the last century, but who feels an irresistible
attraction towards bold metaphysical synthesis !
How rare are such occasions of intellectual
contentment ! This transcendental philosophy,
chiefly as systematised by the mystic Schelling,
Coleridge applied with an eager, unwearied
subtlety, to the questions of theology, and poetic
or artistic criticism. It is in his theory of
poetry, of art, that he comes nearest to principles
of permanent truth and importance : that is the
least fugitive part of his prose work. What,
then, is the essence of his philosophy of art—of
imaginative production ?

Generally, it may be described as an attempt
to reclaim the world of art as a world of fixed
laws, to show that the creative activity of genius
and the simplest act of thought are but higher
and lower products of the laws of a universal
logic. Criticism, feeling its own inadequacy in
dealing with the greater works of art, is sometimes tempted to make too much of those dark
and capricious suggestions of *genius*, which even

74

the intellect possessed by them is unable to explain or recall. It has seemed due to the half-sacred character of those works to ignore all analogy between the productive process by which they had their birth, and the simpler processes of mind. Coleridge, on the other hand, assumes that the highest phases of thought must be more, not less, than the lower, subject to law.

With this interest, in the *Biographia Literaria*, he refines Schelling's "Philosophy of Nature" into a theory of art. "There can be no plagiarism in philosophy," says Heine :—*Es giebt kein Plagiat in der Philosophie*, in reference to the charge brought against Schelling of unacknowledged borrowing from Bruno ; and certainly that which is common to Coleridge and Schelling and Bruno alike is of far earlier origin than any of them. Schellingism, the "Philosophy of Nature," is indeed a constant tradition in the history of thought : it embodies a permanent type of the speculative temper. That mode of conceiving nature as a mirror or reflex of the intelligence of man may be traced up to the first beginnings of Greek speculation. There are two ways of envisaging those aspects of nature which seem to bear the impress of reason or intelligence. There is the deist's way, which regards them merely as marks of design, which separates the informing mind from its result in nature, as the mechanist from the machine ; and there is the pantheistic way, which identifies the two, which regards nature itself as the living energy of an intelligence of the same kind as though vaster in scope than the human. Partly through the influence of mythology, the Greek mind became early possessed with the conception of nature as living, thinking, almost speaking to the mind of man. This unfixed poetical prepossession, reduced to an abstract form, petrified into an idea, is the force which gives unity of aim to Greek philosophy. Little by little, it works out the substance of the Hegelian formula : " Whatever is, is according to reason : whatever is according to reason, that is." Experience, which has gradually saddened the earth's colours for us, stiffened its motions, withdrawn from it some blithe and debonair presence, has quite changed the character of the science of nature, as we understand it. The " positive " method, in truth, makes very little account of marks of intelligence in nature : in its wider view of phenonema, it sees that those instances are a minority, and may rank as happy coincidences : it absorbs them in the larger conception of universal mechanical law. But the suspicion of a mind latent in nature, struggling for release, and intercourse with the intellect of man through true ideas, has never ceased to haunt a certain class of minds. Started again and again in successive periods by enthusiasts on the antique pattern, in each case the thought may have seemed paler and more fantastic amid the grow-

ing consistency and sharpness of outline of other
and more positive forms of knowledge. Still,
wherever the speculative instinct has been united
with a certain poetic inwardness of temperament,
as in Bruno, in Schelling, there that old Greek
conception, like some seed floating in the air,
has taken root and sprung up anew. Coleridge,
thrust inward upon himself, driven from "life in
thought and sensation" to life in thought only,
feels already, in his dark London school, a thread
of the Greek mind on this matter vibrating
strongly in him. At fifteen he is discoursing
on Plotinus, as in later years he reflects from
Schelling that flitting intellectual tradition.
He supposes a subtle, sympathetic co-ordination
between the ideas of the human reason and the
laws of the natural world. Science, the real
knowledge of that natural world, is to be attained,
not by observation, experiment, analysis, patient
generalisation, but by the evolution or recovery
of those ideas directly from within, by a sort
of Platonic "recollection"; every group of
observed facts remaining an enigma until the
appropriate idea is struck upon them from the
mind of a Newton, or a Cuvier, the genius in
whom sympathy with the universal reason becomes entire. In the next place, he conceives
that this reason or intelligence in nature becomes
reflective, or self-conscious. He fancies he can
trace, through all the simpler forms of life,
fragments of an eloquent prophecy about the

human mind. The whole of nature he regards as a development of higher forms out of the lower, through shade after shade of systematic change. The dim stir of chemical atoms towards the axis of crystal form, the trance-like life of plants, the animal troubled by strange irritabilities, are stages which anticipate consciousness. All through the ever-increasing movement of life that was shaping itself; every successive phase of life, in its unsatisfied susceptibilities, seeming to be drawn out of its own limits by the more pronounced current of life on its confines, the "shadow of approaching humanity" gradually deepening, the latent intelligence winning a way to the surface. And at this point the law of development does not lose itself in caprice : rather it becomes more constraining and incisive. From the lowest to the very highest acts of the conscious intelligence, there is another series of refining shades. Gradually the mind concentrates itself, frees itself from the limitations of the particular, the individual, attains a strange power of modifying and centralising what it receives from without, according to the pattern of an inward ideal. At last, in imaginative genius, ideas become effective : the intelligence of nature, all its discursive elements now connected and justified, is clearly reflected ; the interpretation of its latent purposes being embodied in the great central products of creative art. The secret of creative genius would be an exquisitely purged sympathy with nature, with the reasonable soul antecedent there. Those associative conceptions of the imagination, those eternally fixed types of action and passion, would come, not so much from the conscious invention of the artist, as from his self-surrender to the suggestions of an abstract reason or ideality in things : they would be evolved by the stir of nature itself, realising the highest reach of its dormant reason : they would have a kind of prevenient necessity to rise at some time to the surface of the human mind.

It is natural that Shakespeare should be the favourite illustration of such criticism, whether in England or Germany. The first suggestion in Shakespeare is that of capricious detail, of a waywardness that plays with the parts careless of the impression of the whole ; what supervenes is the constraining unity of effect, the ineffaceable impression, of Hamlet or Macbeth. His hand moving freely is curved round as if by some law of gravitation from within : an energetic unity or identity makes itself visible amid an abounding variety. This unity or identity Coleridge exaggerates into something like the identity of a natural organism, and the associative act which effected it into something closely akin to the primitive power of nature itself. " In the Shakespearian drama," he says, "there is a vitality which grows and evolves itself from within."

APPRECIATIONS

Again—

He, too, worked in the spirit of nature, by evolving the germ from within, by the imaginative power, according to the idea. For as the power of seeing is to light, so is an idea in mind to a law in nature. They are correlatives which suppose each other.

Again—

The organic form is innate : it shapes, as it develops, itself from within, and the fulness of its development is one and the same with the perfection of its outward form. Such as the life is, such is the form. Nature, the prime, genial artist, inexhaustible in diverse powers, is equally inexhaustible in forms : each exterior is the physiognomy of the being within, and even such is the appropriate excellence of Shakespeare, himself a nature humanised, a genial understanding, directing self-consciously a power and an implicit wisdom deeper even than our consciousness.

In this late age we are become so familiarised with the greater works of art as to be little sensitive of the act of creation in them : they do not impress us as a new presence in the world. Only sometimes, in productions which realise immediately a profound influence and enforce a change in taste, we are actual witnesses of the moulding of an unforeseen type by some new principle of association ; and to that phenomenon Coleridge wisely recalls our attention. What makes his view a one-sided one is, that in it the artist has become almost a mechanical agent : instead of the most luminous and self-possessed phase of consciousness, the associative act in art or poetry is made to look like some blindly organic process of assimilation. The work of art is likened to a living organism. That ex-

presses truly the sense of a self-delighting, independent life which the finished work of art gives
us : it hardly figures the process by which such
work was produced.   Here there is no blind
ferment of lifeless elements towards the realisation of a type.   By exquisite analysis the artist
attains clearness of idea ; then, through many
stages of refining, clearness of expression.   He
moves slowly over his work, calculating the
tenderest tone, and restraining the subtlest curve,
never letting hand or fancy move at large,
gradually enforcing flaccid spaces to the higher
degree of expressiveness.   The philosophic critic,
at least, will value, even in works of imagination,
seemingly the most intuitive, the power of the
understanding in them, their logical process of
construction, the spectacle of a supreme intellectual dexterity which they afford.

Coleridge's prose writings on philosophy,
politics, religion, and criticism, were, in truth,
but one element in a whole lifetime of endeavours to present the then recent metaphysics
of Germany to English readers, as a legitimate
expansion of the older, classical and native
masters of what has been variously called the
a priori, or absolute, or spiritual, or Platonic, view
of things.   His criticism, his challenge for
recognition in the concrete, visible, finite work
of art, of the dim, unseen, comparatively infinite,
soul or power of the artist, may well be

remembered as part of the long pleading of
German culture for the things "behind the
veil." To introduce that spiritual philosophy,
as represented by the more transcendental parts
of Kant, and by Schelling, into all subjects, as a
system of reason in them, one and ever identical
with itself, however various the matter through
which it was diffused, became with him the
motive of an unflagging enthusiasm, which seems
to have been the one thread of continuity in a life
otherwise singularly wanting in unity of purpose,
and in which he was certainly far from uniformly
at his best. Fragmentary and obscure, but often
eloquent, and always at once earnest and ingenious, those writings, supplementing his remarkable gift of conversation, were directly and
indirectly influential, even on some the furthest
removed from Coleridge's own masters; on
John Stuart Mill, for instance, and some of the
earlier writers of the "high-church" school.
Like his verse, they display him also in two
other characters—as a student of words, and as a
psychologist, that is, as a more minute observer
or student than other men of the phenomena of
mind. To note the recondite associations of
words, old or new; to expound the logic, the
reasonable soul, of their various uses; to recover
the interest of older writers who had had a
phraseology of their own—this was a vein of
inquiry allied to his undoubted gift of tracking
out and analysing curious modes of thought. A

quaint fragment of verse on *Human Life* might serve to illustrate his study of the earlier English philosophical poetry. The latter gift, that power of the "subtle-souled psychologist," as Shelley calls him, seems to have been connected with some tendency to disease in the physical temperament, something of a morbid want of balance in those parts where the physical and intellectual elements mix most closely together, with a kind of languid visionariness, deep-seated in the very constitution of the "narcotist," who had quite a gift for "plucking the poisons of self-harm," and which the actual habit of taking opium, accidentally acquired, did but reinforce. This morbid languor of nature, connected both with his fitfulness of purpose and his rich delicate dreaminess, qualifies Coleridge's poetic composition even more than his prose ; his verse, with the exception of his avowedly political poems, being, unlike that of the "Lake School," to which in some respects he belongs, singularly unaffected by any moral, or professional, or personal effort or ambition,—"written," as he says, "after the more violent emotions of sorrow, to give him pleasure, when perhaps nothing else could ; " but coming thus, indeed, very close to his own most intimately personal characteristics, and having a certain languidly soothing grace or cadence, for its most fixed quality, from first to last. After some Platonic soliloquy on a flower opening on a fine day in February, he goes on—

APPRECIATIONS

Dim similitudes
Weaving in mortal strains, I've stolen one hour
From anxious self, life's cruel taskmaster !
And the warm wooings of this sunny day
Tremble along my frame and harmonise
The attempered organ, that even saddest thoughts
Mix with some sweet sensations, like harsh tunes
Played deftly on a sweet-toned instrument.

The expression of two opposed, yet allied, elements of sensibility in these lines, is very true to Coleridge :—the grievous agitation, the grievous listlessness, almost never entirely relieved, together with a certain physical voluptuousness. He has spoken several times of the scent of the bean-field in the air :—the tropical touches in a chilly climate ; his is a nature that will make the most of these, which finds a sort of caress in such things. *Kubla Khan*, the fragment of a poem actually composed in some certainly not quite healthy sleep, is perhaps chiefly of interest as showing, by the mode of its composition, how physical, how much of a diseased or valetudinarian temperament, in its moments of relief, Coleridge's happiest gift really was ; and side by side with *Kubla Khan* should be read, as Coleridge placed it, the *Pains of Sleep*, to illustrate that retarding physical burden in his temperament, that " unimpassioned grief," the source of which lay so near the source of those pleasures. Connected also with this, and again in contrast with Wordsworth, is the limited quantity of his poetical performance, as he himself regrets so eloquently in the lines addressed to Wordsworth after his recitation of *The Prelude*. It is like some exotic plant, just managing to blossom a little in the somewhat un-english air of Coleridge's own south-western birthplace, but never quite well there.

In 1798 he joined Wordsworth in the composition of a volume of poems—the *Lyrical Ballads*. What Wordsworth then wrote already vibrates with that blithe impulse which carried him to final happiness and self-possession. In Coleridge we feel already that faintness and obscure dejection which clung like some contagious damp to all his work. Wordsworth was to be distinguished by a joyful and penetrative conviction of the existence of certain latent affinities between nature and the human mind, which reciprocally gild the mind and nature with a kind of " heavenly alchemy."

> My voice proclaims
> How exquisitely the individual mind
> (And the progressive powers, perhaps, no less
> Of the whole species) to the external world
> Is fitted ; and how exquisitely, too,
> The external world is fitted to the mind ;
> And the creation, by no lower name
> Can it be called, which they with blended might
> Accomplish.

In Wordsworth this took the form of an unbroken dreaming over the aspects and transitions of nature—a reflective, though altogether unformulated, analysis of them.

There are in Coleridge's poems expressions of this conviction as deep as Wordsworth's. But Coleridge could never have abandoned himself to the dream, the vision, as Wordsworth did, because the first condition of such abandonment must be an unvexed quietness of heart. No one can read the *Lines composed above Tintern* without feeling how potent the physical element was among the conditions of Wordsworth's genius— "felt in the blood and felt along the heart."

> My whole life I have lived in quiet thought!

The stimulus which most artists require of nature he can renounce. He leaves the ready-made glory of the Swiss mountains that he may reflect glory on a mouldering leaf. He loves best to watch the floating thistledown, because of its hint at an unseen life in the air. Coleridge's temperament, ἀεί ἐν σφοδρᾷ ὀρέξει, with its faintness, its grieved dejection, could never have been like that.

> My genial spirits fail;
> And what can these avail
> To lift the smothering weight from off my breast?
> It were a vain endeavour,
> Though I should gaze for ever
> On that green light that lingers in the west:
> I may not hope from outward forms to win
> The passion and the life whose fountains are within.

Wordsworth's flawless temperament, his fine mountain atmosphere of mind, that calm, sabbatic, mystic, wellbeing which De Quincey, a little cynically, connected with worldly (that is to say, pecuniary) good fortune, kept his conviction of a latent intelligence in nature within the limits of sentiment or instinct, and confined it to those delicate and subdued shades of expression which alone perfect art allows. In Coleridge's sadder, more purely intellectual, cast of genius, what with Wordsworth was sentiment or instinct became a philosophical idea, or philosophical formula, developed, as much as possible, after the abstract and metaphysical fashion of the transcendental schools of Germany.

The period of Coleridge's residence at Nether Stowey, 1797-1798, was for him the *annus mirabilis*. Nearly all the chief works by which his poetic fame will live were then composed or planned. What shapes itself for criticism as the main phenomenon of Coleridge's poetic life, is not, as with most true poets, the gradual development of a poetic gift, determined, enriched, retarded, by the actual circumstances of the poet's life, but the sudden blossoming, through one short season, of such a gift already perfect in its kind, which thereafter deteriorates as suddenly, with something like premature old age. Connecting this phenomenon with the leading motive of his prose writings, we might note it as the deterioration of a productive or creative power into one merely metaphysical or discursive. In his unambitious conception of his function as a poet, and in the very limited quantity of his poetical performance, as I have said, he was a contrast to his friend Wordsworth. That friendship with Wordsworth, the chief "developing" circumstance of his poetic life, comprehended a very close intellectual sympathy ; and in such association chiefly, lies whatever truth there may be in the popular classification of Coleridge as a member of what is called the "Lake School." Coleridge's philosophical speculations do really turn on the ideas which underlay Wordsworth's poetical practice. His prose works are one long explanation of all that is involved in that famous distinction between the Fancy and the Imagination. Of what is understood by both writers as the imaginative quality in the use of poetic figures, we may take some words of Shakespeare as an example.—

> My cousin Suffolk,
> My soul shall thine keep company to heaven :
> Tarry, sweet soul, for mine, then fly abreast.

The complete infusion here of the figure into the thought, so vividly realised, that, though birds are not actually mentioned, yet the sense of their flight, conveyed to us by the single word "abreast," comes to be more than half of the thought itself :—this, as the expression of exalted feeling, is an instance of what Coleridge meant by Imagination. And this sort of identification of the poet's thought, of himself, with the image or figure which serves him, is the secret, sometimes, of a singularly entire realisation of that image, such as makes these lines of Coleridge, for instance, " imaginative "—

> Amid the howl of more than wintry storms,
> The halcyon hears the voice of vernal hours
> Already on the wing.

There are many such figures both in Coleridge's verse and prose. He has, too, his passages of that sort of impassioned contemplation on the permanent and elementary conditions of nature and humanity, which Wordsworth held to be the essence of a poet ; as it would be his proper function to awaken such contemplation in other men — those " moments," as Coleridge says, addressing him—

> Moments awful,
> Now in thy inner life, and now abroad,
> When power streamed from thee, and thy soul received
> The light reflected, as a light bestowed.

The entire poem from which these lines are taken, " composed on the night after Wordsworth's recitation of a poem on the growth of an individual mind," is, in its high-pitched strain of meditation, and in the combined justice and elevation of its philosophical expression—

> high and passionate thoughts
> To their own music chanted ;

wholly sympathetic with *The Prelude* which it celebrates, and of which the subject is, in effect, the generation of the spirit of the " Lake poetry."

APPRECIATIONS

The *Lines to Joseph Cottle* have the same philo-sophically imaginative character ; the *Ode to Dejection* being Coleridge's most sustained effort of this kind.

It is in a highly sensitive apprehension of the aspects of external nature that Coleridge identi-fies himself most closely with one of the main tendencies of the " Lake School " ; a tendency instinctive, and no mere matter of theory, in him as in Wordsworth.   That record of the

> green light
> Which lingers in the west,

and again, of

> the western sky,
> And its peculiar tint of yellow green,

which Byron found ludicrously untrue, but which surely needs no defence, is a characteristic example of a singular watchfulness for the minute fact and expression of natural scenery pervading all he wrote—a closeness to the exact physiognomy of nature, having something to do with that idealistic philosophy which sees in the external world no mere concurrence of mechanical agencies, but an animated body, informed and made expressive, like the body of man, by an indwelling intelligence.   It was a tendency, doubtless, in the air, for Shelley too is affected by it, and Turner, with the school of landscape which followed him.   " I had found," Coleridge tells us,

That outward forms, the loftiest, still receive
Their finer influence from the world within ;
Fair ciphers of vague import, where the eye
Traces no spot, in which the heart may read
History and prophecy : . . .

and this induces in him no indifference to actual colour and form and process, but such minute realism as this—

The thin grey cloud is spread on high,
It covers but not hides the sky.
The moon is behind and at the full ;
And yet she looks both small and dull ;

or this, which has a touch of " romantic " weirdness—

Nought was green upon the oak
But moss and rarest misletoe :

or this—

There is not wind enough to twirl
The one red leaf, the last of its clan,
That dances as often as dance it can,
Hanging so light, and hanging so high,
On the topmost twig that looks up at the sky :

or this, with a weirdness, again, like that of some wild French etcher—

Lo ! the new-moon winter-bright !
And overspread with phantom light
(With swimming phantom light o'erspread,
But rimmed and circled with a silver thread)
I see the old moon in her lap, foretelling
The coming on of rain and squally blast.

He has a like imaginative apprehension of the silent and unseen processes of nature, its " minis-

APPRECIATIONS

tries" of dew and frost, for instance ; as when
he writes, in April—

> A balmy night ! and though the stars be dim,
> Yet let us think upon the vernal showers
> That gladden the green earth, and we shall find
> A pleasure in the dimness of the stars.

Of such imaginative treatment of landscape there
is no better instance than the description of *The
Dell*, in *Fears in Solitude*—

> A green and silent spot amid the hills,
> A small and silent dell ! O'er stiller place
> No singing skylark ever poised himself—
> But the dell,
> Bathed by the mist is fresh and delicate
> As vernal cornfield, or the unripe flax
> When, through its half-transparent stalks, at eve,
> The level sunshine glimmers with green light :—
> The gust that roared and died away
> To the distant tree—
> heard and only heard
> In this low dell, bowed not the delicate grass.

This curious insistence of the mind on one
particular spot, till it seems to attain actual expression and a sort of soul in it—a mood so
characteristic of the " Lake School "—occurs in
an earnest political poem, "written in April
1798, during the alarm of an invasion " ; and
that silent dell is the background against which
the tumultuous fears of the poet are in strong
relief, while the quiet sense of the place, maintained all through them, gives a true poetic
unity to the piece. Good political poetry—

political poetry that shall be permanently moving — can, perhaps, only be written on motives
which, for those they concern, have ceased to be
open questions, and are really beyond argument ;
while Coleridge's political poems are for the
most part on open questions. For although it
was a great part of his intellectual ambition to
subject political questions to the action of the
fundamental ideas of his philosophy, he was
nevertheless an ardent partisan, first on one side,
then on the other, of the actual politics proper
to the end of the last and the beginning of the
present century, where there is still room for
much difference of opinion. Yet *The Destiny of
Nations*, though formless as a whole, and un-
finished, presents many traces of his most elevated
manner of speculation, cast into that sort of
imaginative philosophical expression, in which,
in effect, the language itself is inseparable from,
or essentially a part of, the thought. *France,
an Ode*, begins with a famous apostrophe to
Liberty—

Ye Clouds ! that far above me float and pause,
    Whose pathless march no mortal may control !
Ye Ocean-waves ! that wheresoe'er ye roll,
Yield homage only to eternal laws !
Ye Woods ! that listen to the night-bird's singing,
    Midway the smooth and perilous slope reclined,
Save when your own imperious branches swinging,
    Have made a solemn music of the wind !
Where like a man beloved of God,
Through glooms which never woodman trod,
    How oft, pursuing fancies holy,

APPRECIATIONS

My moonlight way o'er flowering weeds I wound,
Inspired, beyond the guess of folly,
By each rude shape and wild unconquerable sound !
O ye loud Waves ! and O ye Forests high !
    And O ye Clouds that far above me soar'd !
Thou rising Sun ! thou blue rejoicing Sky !
Yea, everything that is and will be free !
Bear witness for me, wheresoe'er ye be,
With what deep worship I have still adored
    The spirit of divinest liberty.

And the whole ode, though, after Coleridge's
way, not quite equal to that *exordium*, is an
example of strong national sentiment, partly in
indignant reaction against his own earlier sympathy with the French Republic, inspiring a
composition which, in spite of some turgid lines,
really justifies itself as poetry, and has that true
unity of effect which the ode requires.   Liberty,
after all his hopes of young France, is only to be
found in nature :—

    Thou speedest on thy subtle pinions,
The guide of homeless winds, and playmate of the waves !

In his changes of political sentiment, Coleridge
was associated with the " Lake School " ; and
there is yet one other very different sort of
sentiment in which he is one with that school,
yet all himself, his sympathy, namely, with the
animal world.   That was a sentiment connected
at once with the love of outward nature in
himself and in the " Lake School," and its assertion of the natural affections in their simplicity ;
with the homeliness and pity, consequent upon

94

that assertion. The *Lines to a Young Ass*, tethered—

> Where the close-eaten grass is scarcely seen,
> While sweet around her waves the tempting green,

which had seemed merely whimsical in their day, indicate a vein of interest constant in Coleridge's poems, and at its height in his greatest poems—in *Christabel*, where it has its effect, as it were antipathetically, in the vivid realisation of the serpentine element in Geraldine's nature ; and in *The Ancient Mariner*, whose fate is interwoven with that of the wonderful bird, at whose blessing of the water-snakes the curse for the death of the albatross passes away, and where the moral of the love of all creatures, as a sort of religious duty, is definitely expressed.

Christabel, though not printed till 1816, was written mainly in the year 1797 : *The Rhyme of the Ancient Mariner* was printed as a contribution to the *Lyrical Ballads* in 1798 ; and these two poems belong to the great year of Coleridge's poetic production, his twenty-fifth year. In poetic quality, above all in that most poetic of all qualities, a keen sense of, and delight in beauty, the infection of which lays hold upon the reader, they are quite out of proportion to all his other compositions. The form in both is that of the ballad, with some of its terminology, and some also of its quaint conceits. They connect themselves with that revival of ballad litera-ture, of which Percy's *Relics*, and, in another way, Macpherson's *Ossian* are monuments, and which afterwards so powerfully affected Scott—

> Young-eyed poesy
> All deftly masked as hoar antiquity.

The Ancient Mariner, as also, in its measure, *Christabel*, is a "romantic" poem, impressing us by bold invention, and appealing to that taste for the supernatural, that longing for *le frisson*, a shudder, to which the "romantic" school in Germany, and its derivations in England and France, directly ministered. In Coleridge, personally, this taste had been encouraged by his odd and out-of-the-way reading in the old-fashioned literature of the marvellous—books like Purchas's *Pilgrims*, early voyages like Hakluyt's, old naturalists and visionary moralists, like Thomas Burnet, from whom he quotes the motto of *The Ancient Mariner*, "*Facile credo, plures esse naturas invisibiles quam visibiles in rerum universitate, etc.*" Fancies of the strange things which may very well happen, even in broad daylight, to men shut up alone in ships far off on the sea, seem to have occurred to the human mind in all ages with a peculiar readiness, and often have about them, from the story of the stealing of Dionysus downwards, the fascination of a certain dreamy grace, which distinguishes them from other kinds of marvellous inventions. This sort of fascination *The Ancient Mariner* brings to its highest degree : it is the delicacy, the dreamy grace, in his presentation of the marvellous, which makes Coleridge's work so remarkable. The too palpable intruders from a spiritual world in almost all ghost literature, in Scott and Shakespeare even, have a kind of crudity or coarseness. Coleridge's power is in the very fineness with which, as by some really ghostly finger, he brings home to our inmost sense his inventions, daring as they are—the skeleton ship, the polar spirit, the inspiriting of the dead corpses of the ship's crew. *The Rhyme of the Ancient Mariner* has the plausibility, the perfect adaptation to reason and the general aspect of life, which belongs to the marvellous, when actually presented as part of a credible experience in our dreams. Doubtless, the mere experience of the opium-eater, the habit he must almost necessarily fall into of noting the more elusive phenomena of dreams, had something to do with that : in its essence, however, it is connected with a more purely intellectual circumstance in the development of Coleridge's poetic gift. Some one once asked William Blake, to whom Coleridge has many resemblances, when either is at his best (that whole episode of the re-inspiriting of the ship's crew in *The Ancient Mariner* being comparable to Blake's well-known design of the " Morning Stars singing together ") whether he had ever seen a ghost, and was surprised when the famous seer, who ought, one might think, to have seen so many, answered frankly, " Only

once ! " His " spirits," at once more delicate,
and so much more real, than any ghost—the
burden, as they were the privilege, of his *temperament*—like it, were an integral element in his
everyday life. And the difference of mood
expressed in that question and its answer, is
indicative of a change of temper in regard to
the supernatural which has passed over the
whole modern mind, and of which the true
measure is the influence of the writings of
Swedenborg. What that change is we may see
if we compare the vision by which Swedenborg
was " called," as he thought, to his work, with
the ghost which called Hamlet, or the spells of
Marlowe's *Faust* with those of Goethe's. The
modern mind, so minutely self-scrutinising, if it
is to be affected at all by a sense of the supernatural, needs to be more finely touched than
was possible in the older, romantic presentment
of it. The spectral object, so crude, so impossible,
has become plausible, as

> The blot upon the brain,
> That *will* show itself without ;

and is understood to be but a condition of one's
own mind, for which, according to the scepticism,
latent at least, in so much of our modern philosophy, the so-called real things themselves are
but *spectra* after all.

It is this finer, more delicately marvellous
supernaturalism, fruit of his more delicate

psychology, that Coleridge infuses into romantic adventure, itself also then a new or revived thing in English literature ; and with a fineness of weird effect in *The Ancient Mariner*, unknown in those older, more simple, romantic legends and ballads. It is a flower of medieval or later German romance, growing up in the peculiarly compounded atmosphere of modern psychological speculation, and putting forth in it wholly new qualities. The quaint prose commentary, which runs side by side with the verse of *The Ancient Mariner*, illustrates this—a composition of quite a different shade of beauty and merit from that of the verse which it accompanies, connecting this, the chief poem of Coleridge, with his philosophy, and emphasising therein that psychological interest of which I have spoken, its curious soul-lore.

Completeness, the perfectly rounded wholeness and unity of the impression it leaves on the mind of a reader who fairly gives himself to it— that, too, is one of the characteristics of a really excellent work, in the poetic as in every other kind of art ; and by this completeness, *The Ancient Mariner* certainly gains upon *Christabel* —a completeness, entire as that of Wordsworth's *Leech-gatherer*, or Keats's *Saint Agnes' Eve*, each typical in its way of such wholeness or entirety of effect on a careful reader. It is Coleridge's one great complete work, the one really finished thing, in a life of many beginnings. *Christabel* remained a fragment. In *The Ancient Mariner* this unity is secured in part by the skill with which the incidents of the marriage-feast are made to break in dreamily from time to time upon the main story. And then, how pleasantly, how reassuringly, the whole nightmare story itself is made to end, among the clear fresh sounds and lights of the bay, where it began, with

> The moon-light steeped in silentness,
> The steady weather-cock.

So different from *The Rhyme of the Ancient Mariner* in regard to this completeness of effect, *Christabel* illustrates the same complexion of motives, a like intellectual situation. Here, too, the work is of a kind peculiar to one who touches the characteristic motives of the old romantic ballad, with a spirit made subtle and fine by modern reflection ; as we feel, I think, in such passages as—

> But though my slumber had gone by,
> This dream it would not pass away—
> It seems to live upon mine eye ;—

and—

> For she, belike, hath drunken deep
> Of all the blessedness of sleep ;

and again—

> With such perplexity of mind
> As dreams too lively leave behind.

And that gift of handling the finer passages of human feeling, at once with power and delicacy, which was another result of his finer psychology,

of his exquisitely refined habit of self-reflection,
is illustrated by a passage on Friendship in the
Second Part—

> Alas ! they had been friends in youth ;
> But whispering tongues can poison truth ;
> And constancy lives in realms above ;
> And life is thorny ; and youth is vain ;
> And to be wroth with one we love,
> Doth work like madness in the brain.
> And thus it chanced, as I divine,
> With Roland and Sir Leoline.
> Each spake words of high disdain
> And insult to his heart's best brother :
> They parted—ne'er to meet again !
> But never either found another
> To free the hollow heart from paining—
> They stood aloof the scars remaining,
> Like cliffs which had been rent asunder ;
> A dreary sea now flows between ;
> But neither heat, nor frost, nor thunder,
> Shall wholly do away, I ween,
> The marks of that which once hath been.

I suppose these lines leave almost every reader
with a quickened sense of the beauty and compass of human feeling ; and it is the sense of
such richness and beauty which, in spite of his
" dejection," in spite of that burden of his morbid
lassitude, accompanies Coleridge himself through
life. A warm poetic joy in everything beautiful,
whether it be a moral sentiment, like the friendship of Roland and Leoline, or only the flakes of
falling light from the water-snakes—this joy,
visiting him, now and again, after sickly dreams,
in sleep or waking, as a relief not to be for-

gotten, and with such a power of felicitous expression that the infection of it passes irresistibly
to the reader—such is the predominant element
in the matter of his poetry, as cadence is the
predominant quality of its form. " We bless
thee for our creation ! " he might have said,
in his later period of definite religious assent,
" because the world is so beautiful : the world of
ideas—living spirits, detached from the divine
nature itself, to inform and lift the heavy mass
of material things ; the world of man, above all
in his melodious and intelligible speech ; the
world of living creatures and natural scenery ;
the world of dreams." What he really did say,
by way of *A Tombless Epitaph*, is true enough of
himself—

> Sickness, 'tis true,
> Whole years of weary days, besieged him close,
> Even to the gates and inlets of his life !
> But it is true, no less, that strenuous, firm,
> And with a natural gladness, he maintained
> The citadel unconquered, and in joy
> Was strong to follow the delightful Muse.
> For not a hidden path, that to the shades
> Of the beloved Parnassian forest leads,
> Lurked undiscovered by him ; not a rill
> There issues from the fount of Hippocrene,
> But he had traced it upward to its source,
> Through open glade, dark glen, and secret dell,
> Knew the gay wild flowers on its banks, and culled
> Its med'cinable herbs. Yea, oft alone,
> Piercing the long-neglected holy cave,
> The haunt obscure of old Philosophy,
> He bade with lifted torch its starry walls
> Sparkle, as erst they sparkled to the flame

COLERIDGE

Of odorous lamps tended by saint and sage.
O framed for calmer times and nobler hearts !
O studious Poet, eloquent for truth !
Philosopher ! contemning wealth and death,
Yet docile, childlike, full of Life and Love.

The student of empirical science asks, Are absolute principles attainable ? What are the limits of knowledge ? The answer he receives from science itself is not ambiguous. What the moralist asks is, Shall we gain or lose by surrendering human life to the relative spirit ? Experience answers that the dominant tendency of life is to turn ascertained truth into a dead letter, to make us all the phlegmatic servants of routine. The relative spirit, by its constant dwelling on the more fugitive conditions or circumstances of things, breaking through a thousand rough and brutal classifications, and giving elasticity to inflexible principles, begets an intellectual *finesse* of which the ethical result is a delicate and tender justice in the criticism of human life. Who would gain more than Coleridge by criticism in such a spirit ? We know how his life has appeared when judged by absolute standards. We see him trying to "apprehend the absolute," to stereotype forms of faith and philosophy, to attain, as he says, "fixed principles" in politics, morals, and religion, to fix one mode of life as the essence of life, refusing to see the parts as parts only ; and all the time his own pathetic history pleads for a more elastic moral philosophy than his, and cries out against every formula less living and flexible than life itself.

"From his childhood he hungered for eternity." There, after all, is the incontestable claim of Coleridge. The perfect flower of any elementary type of life must always be precious to humanity, and Coleridge is a true flower of the *ennuyé*, of the type of René. More than Childe Harold, more than Werther, more than René himself, Coleridge, by what he did, what he was, and what he failed to do, represents that inexhaustible discontent, languor, and home-sickness, that endless regret, the chords of which ring all through our modern literature. It is to the romantic element in literature that those qualities belong. One day, perhaps, we may come to forget the distant horizon, with full knowledge of the situation, to be content with " what is here and now " ; and herein is the essence of classical feeling. But by us of the present moment, certainly—by us for whom the Greek spirit, with its engaging naturalness, simple, chastened, debonair, τρυφῆς, ἀβρότητος, χλιδῆς, χαρίτων, ἱμέρου, πόθου πατήρ, is itself the Sangrail of an endless pilgrimage, Coleridge, with his passion for the absolute, for something fixed where all is moving, his faintness, his broken memory, his intellectual disquiet, may still be ranked among the interpreters of one of the constituent elements of our life.

1865, 1880.

CHARLES LAMB

THOSE English critics who at the beginning of the present century introduced from Germany, together with some other subtleties of thought transplanted hither not without advantage, the distinction between the *Fancy* and the *Imagination*, made much also of the cognate distinction between *Wit* and *Humour*, between that unreal and transitory mirth, which is as the crackling of thorns under the pot, and the laughter which blends with tears and even with the sublimities of the imagination, and which, in its most exquisite motives, is one with pity—the laughter of the comedies of Shakespeare, hardly less expressive than his moods of seriousness or solemnity, of that deeply stirred soul of sympathy in him, as flowing from which both tears and laughter are alike genuine and contagious.

This distinction between wit and humour, Coleridge and other kindred critics applied, with much effect, in their studies of some of our older English writers. And as the distinction between imagination and fancy, made popular by Words-

worth, found its best justification in certain
essential differences of stuff in Wordsworth's
own writings, so this other critical distinction,
between wit and humour, finds a sort of visible
interpretation and instance in the character and
writings of Charles Lamb ;—one who lived more
consistently than most writers among subtle
literary theories, and whose remains are still
full of curious interest for the student of literature
as a fine art.

The author of the *English Humourists of the
Eighteenth Century*, coming to the humourists of
the nineteenth, would have found, as is true pre-
eminently of Thackeray himself, the springs of
pity in them deepened by the deeper subjectivity,
the intenser and closer living with itself, which
is characteristic of the temper of the later
generation ; and therewith, the mirth also, from
the amalgam of which with pity humour proceeds, has become, in Charles Dickens, for
example, freer and more boisterous.

To this more high-pitched feeling, since
predominant in our literature, the writings of
Charles Lamb, whose life occupies the last
quarter of the eighteenth century and the first
quarter of the nineteenth, are a transition ; and
such union of grave, of terrible even, with gay,
we may note in the circumstances of his life, as
reflected thence into his work. We catch the
aroma of a singular, homely sweetness about his
first years, spent on Thames' side, amid the red

bricks and terraced gardens, with their rich historical memories of old-fashioned legal London. Just above the poorer class, deprived, as he says, of the " sweet food of academic institution," he is fortunate enough to be reared in the classical languages at an ancient school, where he becomes the companion of Coleridge, as at a later period he was his enthusiastic disciple. So far, the years go by with less than the usual share of boyish difficulties ; protected, one fancies, seeing what he was afterwards, by some attraction of temper in the quaint child, small and delicate, with a certain Jewish expression in his clear, brown complexion, eyes not precisely of the same colour, and a slow walk adding to the staidness of his figure ; and whose infirmity of speech, increased by agitation, is partly engaging.

And the cheerfulness of all this, of the mere aspect of Lamb's quiet subsequent life also, might make the more superficial reader think of him as in himself something slight, and of his mirth as cheaply bought. Yet we know that beneath this blithe surface there was something of the fateful domestic horror, of the beautiful heroism and devotedness too, of old Greek tragedy. His sister Mary, ten years his senior, in a sudden paroxysm of madness, caused the death of her mother, and was brought to trial for what an overstrained justice might have construed as the greatest of crimes. She was released on the brother's pledging himself to watch over her ; and to this sister, from the age of twenty-one, Charles Lamb sacrificed himself, "seeking thenceforth," says his earliest biographer, "no connexion which could interfere with her supremacy in his affections, or impair his ability to sustain and comfort her." The "feverish, romantic tie of love," he cast away in exchange for the "charities of home." Only, from time to time, the madness returned, affecting him too, once ; and we see the brother and sister voluntarily yielding to restraint. In estimating the humour of *Elia*, we must no more forget the strong undercurrent of this great misfortune and pity, than one could forget it in his actual story. So he becomes the best critic, almost the discoverer, of Webster, a dramatist of genius so sombre, so heavily coloured, so *macabre*. *Rosamund Grey*, written in his twenty-third year, a story with something bitter and exaggerated, an almost insane fixedness of gloom perceptible in it, strikes clearly this note in his work.

For himself, and from his own point of view, the exercise of his gift, of his literary art, came to gild or sweeten a life of monotonous labour, and seemed, as far as regarded others, no very important thing ; availing to give them a little pleasure, and inform them a little, chiefly in a retrospective manner, but in no way concerned with the turning of the tides of the great world. And yet this very modesty, this unambitious way of conceiving his work, has impressed upon it a certain exceptional enduringness. For of the remarkable English writers contemporary with Lamb, many were greatly preoccupied with ideas of practice—religious, moral, political —ideas which have since, in some sense or other, entered permanently into the general consciousness ; and, these having no longer any stimulus for a generation provided with a different stock of ideas, the writings of those who spent so much of themselves in their propagation have lost, with posterity, something of what they gained by them in immediate influence. Coleridge, Wordsworth, Shelley even—sharing so largely in the unrest of their own age, and made personally more interesting thereby, yet, of their actual work, surrender more to the mere course of time than some of those who may have seemed to exercise themselves hardly at all in great matters, to have been little serious, or a little indifferent, regarding them.

Of this number of the disinterested servants of literature, smaller in England than in France, Charles Lamb is one. In the making of prose he realises the principle of art for its own sake, as completely as Keats in the making of verse. And, working ever close to the concrete, to the details, great or small, of actual things, books, persons, and with no part of them blurred to his vision by the intervention of mere abstract theories, he has reached an enduring moral effect

APPRECIATIONS

also, in a sort of boundless sympathy. Unoc-
cupied, as he might seem, with great matters,
he is in immediate contact with what is real,
especially in its caressing littleness, that littleness in which there is much of the whole woeful
heart of things, and meets it more than half-way
with a perfect understanding of it. What sudden,
unexpected touches of pathos in him !—bearing
witness how the sorrow of humanity, the *Welt-
schmerz*, the constant aching of its wounds, is
ever present with him : but what a gift also
for the enjoyment of life in its subtleties, of enjoyment actually refined by the need of some
thoughtful economies and making the most of
things ! Little arts of happiness he is ready to
teach to others. The quaint remarks of children
which another would scarcely have heard, he
preserves—little flies in the priceless amber of
his Attic wit—and has his " Praise of chimney-
sweepers " (as William Blake has written, with
so much natural pathos, the Chimney-sweeper's
Song) valuing carefully their white teeth, and
fine enjoyment of white sheets in stolen sleep at
Arundel Castle, as he tells the story, anticipating
something of the mood of our deep humourists
of the last generation. His simple mother-pity
for those who suffer by accident, or unkindness
of nature, blindness for instance, or fateful disease
of mind like his sister's, has something primitive in its largeness ; and on behalf of ill-used
animals he is early in composing a *Pity's Gift*.

CHARLES LAMB

And if, in deeper or more superficial sense, the dead *do* care at all for their name and fame, then how must the souls of Shakespeare and Webster have been stirred, after so long converse with things that stopped their ears, whether above or below the soil, at his exquisite appreciations of them ; the souls of Titian and of Hogarth too ; for, what has not been observed so generally as the excellence of his literary criticism, Charles Lamb is a fine critic of painting also. It was as loyal, self-forgetful work for others, for Shakespeare's self first, for instance, and then for Shakespeare's readers, that that too was done : he has the true scholar's way of forgetting himself in his subject. For though " defrauded," as we saw, in his young years, " of the sweet food of academic institution," he is yet essentially a scholar, and all his work mainly retrospective, as I said ; his own sorrows, affections, perceptions, being alone real to him of the present. " I cannot make these present times," he says once, " present to *me*."

Above all, he becomes not merely an expositor, permanently valuable, but for Englishmen almost the discoverer of the old English drama. " The book is such as I am glad there should be," he modestly says of the *Specimens of English Dramatic Poets who lived about the time of Shakespeare* ; to which, however, he adds in a series of notes the very quintessence of criticism, the choicest savour and perfume of Elizabethan poetry being sorted, and stored here, with a sort of delicate intellectual epicureanism, which has had the effect of winning for these, then almost forgotten, poets, one generation after another of enthusiastic students. Could he but have known how fresh a source of culture he was evoking there for other generations, through all those years in which, a little wistfully, he would harp on the limitation of his time by business, and sigh for a better fortune in regard to literary opportunities!

To feel strongly the charm of an old poet or moralist, the literary charm of Burton, for instance, or Quarles, or The Duchess of New-castle; and then to interpret that charm, to convey it to others—he seeming to himself but to hand on to others, in mere humble ministra-tion, that of which for them he is really the creator—this is the way of his criticism; cast off in a stray letter often, or passing note, or lightest essay or conversation. It is in such a letter, for instance, that we come upon a singularly penetrative estimate of the genius and writings of Defoe.

Tracking, with an attention always alert, the whole process of their production to its starting-point in the deep places of the mind, he seems to realise the but half-conscious intuitions of Hogarth or Shakespeare, and develops the great ruling unities which have swayed their actual work; or "puts up," and takes, the one morsel of good stuff in an old, forgotten writer. Even

in what he says casually there comes an aroma
of old English ; noticeable echoes, in chance
turn and phrase, of the great masters of style,
the old masters. Godwin, seeing in quotation
a passage from *John Woodvil*, takes it for a choice
fragment of an old dramatist, and goes to Lamb
to assist him in finding the author. His power
of delicate imitation in prose and verse reaches
the length of a fine mimicry even, as in those
last essays of Elia on Popular Fallacies, with their
gentle reproduction or caricature of Sir Thomas
Browne, showing, the more completely, his
mastery, by disinterested study, of those elements
of the man which were the real source of style
in that great, solemn master of old English, who,
ready to say what he has to say with fearless
homeliness, yet continually overawes one with
touches of a strange utterance from worlds afar.
For it is with the delicacies of fine literature
especially, its gradations of expression, its fine
judgment, its pure sense of words, of vocabulary
—things, alas ! dying out in the English literature
of the present, together with the appreciation of
them in our literature of the past—that his literary
mission is chiefly concerned. And yet, delicate,
refining, daintily epicurean, as he may seem,
when he writes of giants, such as Hogarth or
Shakespeare, though often but in a stray note,
you catch the sense of veneration with which
those great names in past literature and art
brooded over his intelligence, his undiminished

impressibility by the great effects in them. Reading, commenting on Shakespeare, he is like a man who walks alone under a grand stormy sky, and among unwonted tricks of light, when powerful spirits might seem to be abroad upon the air ; and the grim humour of Hogarth, as he analyses it, rises into a kind of spectral grotesque ; while he too knows the secret of fine, significant touches like theirs.

There are traits, customs, characteristics of houses and dress, surviving morsels of old life, such as Hogarth has transferred so vividly into *The Rake's Progress*, or *Marriage à la Mode*, concerning which we well understand how, common, uninteresting, or even worthless in themselves, they have come to please us at last as things picturesque, being set in relief against the modes of our different age. Customs, stiff to us, stiff dresses, stiff furniture—types of cast-off fashions, left by accident, and which no one ever meant to preserve—we contemplate with more than good-nature, as having in them the veritable accent of a time, not altogether to be replaced by its more solemn and self-conscious deposits ; like those tricks of individuality which we find quite tolerable in persons, because they convey to us the secret of lifelike expression, and with regard to which we are all to some extent humourists. But it is part of the privilege of the genuine humourist to anticipate this pensive mood with regard to the ways and things

of his own day ; to look upon the tricks in
manner of the life about him with that same
refined, purged sort of vision, which will come
naturally to those of a later generation, in observing whatever may have survived by chance
of its mere external habit. Seeing things always
by the light of an understanding more entire
than is possible for ordinary minds, of the whole
mechanism of humanity, and seeing also the
manner, the outward mode or fashion, always
in strict connexion with the spiritual condition which determined it, a humourist such as
Charles Lamb anticipates the enchantment of
distance ; and the characteristics of places, ranks,
habits of life, are transfigured for him, even now
and in advance of time, by poetic light ; justifying what some might condemn as mere senti-
mentality, in the effort to hand on unbroken
the tradition of such fashion or accent. " The
praise of beggars," " the cries of London," the
traits of actors just grown " old," the spots in
" town " where the country, its fresh green and
fresh water, still lingered on, one after another,
amidst the bustle ; the quaint, dimmed, just
played-out farces, he had relished so much,
coming partly through them to understand the
earlier English theatre as a thing once really
alive ; those fountains and sun-dials of old
gardens, of which he entertains such dainty
discourse :—he feels the poetry of these things,
as the poetry of things old indeed, but surviving

as an actual part of the life of the present, and as something quite different from the poetry of things flatly gone from us and antique, which come back to us, if at all, as entire strangers, like Scott's old Scotch-border personages, their oaths and armour. Such gift of appreciation depends, as I said, on the habitual apprehension of men's life as a whole—its organic wholeness, as extending even to the least things in it—of its outward manner in connexion with its inward temper ; and it involves a fine perception of the congruities, the musical accordance between humanity and its environment of custom, society, personal intercourse ; as if all this, with its meetings, partings, ceremonies, gesture, tones of speech, were some delicate instrument on which an expert performer is playing.

These are some of the characteristics of Elia, one essentially an essayist, and of the true family of Montaigne, "never judging," as he says, " system-wise of things, but fastening on particulars ; " saying all things as it were on chance occasion only, and by way of pastime, yet succeeding thus, " glimpse-wise," in catching and recording more frequently than others " the gayest, happiest attitude of things ; " a casual writer for dreamy readers, yet always giving the reader so much more than he seemed to propose. There is something of the follower of George Fox about him, and the Quaker's belief in the inward light coming to one passive,

to the mere wayfarer, who will be sure at all
events to lose no light which falls by the way—
glimpses, suggestions, delightful half-apprehen-
sions, profound thoughts of old philosophers,
hints of the innermost reason in things, the full
knowledge of which is held in reserve ; all the
varied stuff, that is, of which genuine essays are
made.

And with him, as with Montaigne, the desire
of self-portraiture is, below all more superficial
tendencies, the real motive in writing at all—a
desire closely connected with that intimacy, that
modern subjectivity, which may be called the
Montaignesque element in literature. What he
designs is to give you himself, to acquaint you
with his likeness ; but must do this, if at all,
indirectly, being indeed always more or less
reserved, for himself and his friends ; friendship
counting for so much in his life, that he is
jealous of anything that might jar or disturb it,
even to the length of a sort of insincerity, to
which he assigns its quaint " praise " ; this lover
of stage plays significantly welcoming a little
touch of the artificiality of play to sweeten the
intercourse of actual life.

And, in effect, a very delicate and expressive
portrait of him does put itself together for the
duly meditative reader. In indirect touches of
his own work, scraps of faded old letters, what
others remembered of his talk, the man's likeness emerges ; what he laughed and wept at,

his sudden elevations, and longings after absent friends, his fine casuistries of affection and devices to jog sometimes, as he says, the lazy happiness of perfect love, his solemn moments of higher discourse with the young, as they came across him on occasion, and went along a little way with him, the sudden, surprised apprehension of beauties in old literature, revealing anew the deep soul of poetry in things, and withal the pure spirit of fun, having its way again ; laughter, that most short-lived of all things (some of Shakespeare's even being grown hollow) wearing well with him. Much of all this comes out through his letters, which may be regarded as a department of his essays. He is an old-fashioned letter-writer, the essence of the old fashion of letter-writing lying, as with true essay-writing, in the dexterous availing oneself of accident and circumstance, in the prosecution of deeper lines of observation ; although, just as with the record of his conversation, one loses something, in losing the actual tones of the stammerer, still graceful in his halting, as he halted also in composition, composing slowly and by fits, "like a Flemish painter," as he tells us, so "it is to be regretted," says the editor of his letters, "that in the printed letters the reader will lose the curious varieties of writing with which the originals abound, and which are scrupulously adapted to the subject."

Also, he was a true "collector," delighting

in the personal finding of a thing, in the colour
an old book or print gets for him by the
little accidents which attest previous ownership.
Wither's *Emblems*, "that old book and quaint,"
long-desired, when he finds it at last, he values
none the less because a child had coloured the
plates with his paints. A lover of household
warmth everywhere, of that tempered atmosphere
which our various habitations get by men's living
within them, he "sticks to his favourite books
as he did to his friends," and loved the "town,"
with a jealous eye for all its characteristics, "old
houses" coming to have souls for him. The
yearning for mere warmth against him in another,
makes him content, all through life, with pure
brotherliness, "the most kindly and natural
species of love," as he says, in place of the
passion of love. Brother and sister, sitting thus
side by side, have, of course, their anticipations
how one of them must sit at last in the faint sun
alone, and set us speculating, as we read, as to
precisely what amount of melancholy really
accompanied for him the approach of old age,
so steadily foreseen ; make us note also, with
pleasure, his successive wakings up to cheerful realities, out of a too curious musing over
what is gone and what remains, of life. In his
subtle capacity for enjoying the more refined
points of earth, of human relationship, he could
throw the gleam of poetry or humour on what
seemed common or threadbare ; has a care for the

sighs, and the weary, humdrum preoccupations
of very weak people, down to their little pathetic
" gentilities," even ; while, in the purely human
temper, he can write of death, almost like Shakespeare.

And that care, through all his enthusiasm of
discovery, for what is accustomed, in literature,
connected thus with his close clinging to home
and the earth, was congruous also with that love
for the accustomed in religion, which we may
notice in him. He is one of the last votaries
of that old-world sentiment, based on the feelings
of hope and awe, which may be described as the
religion of men of letters (as Sir Thomas Browne
has his *Religion of the Physician*) religion as understood by the soberer men of letters in the last
century, Addison, Gray, and Johnson ; by Jane
Austen and Thackeray, later. A high way of
feeling developed largely by constant intercourse
with the great things of literature, and extended
in its turn to those matters greater still, this
religion lives, in the main retrospectively, in
a system of received sentiments and beliefs ;
received, like those great things of literature and
art, in the first instance, on the authority of a
long tradition, in the course of which they have
linked themselves in a thousand complex ways
to the conditions of human life, and no more
questioned now than the feeling one keeps by
one of the greatness—say ! of Shakespeare. For
Charles Lamb, such form of religion becomes

the solemn background on which the nearer
and more exciting objects of his immediate
experience relieve themselves, borrowing from
it an expression of calm ; its necessary atmosphere being indeed a profound quiet, that quiet
which has in it a kind of sacramental efficacy,
working, we might say, on the principle of the
opus operatum, almost without any co-operation
of one's own, towards the assertion of the higher
self.   And, in truth, to men of Lamb's delicately
attuned temperament mere physical stillness has
its full value ; such natures seeming to long for
it sometimes, as for no merely negative thing,
with a sort of mystical sensuality.

The writings of Charles Lamb are an excellent illustration of the value of reserve in literature.   Below his quiet, his quaintness, his humour,
and what may seem the slightness, the occasional
or accidental character of his work, there lies, as
I said at starting, as in his life, a genuinely tragic
element.   The gloom, reflected at its darkest in
those hard shadows of *Rosamund Grey*, is always
there, though not always realised either for himself or his readers, and restrained always in
utterance.   It gives to those lighter matters on
the surface of life and literature among which
he for the most part moved, a wonderful force
of expression, as if at any moment these slight
words and fancies might pierce very far into the
deeper soul of things.   In his writing, as in his

life, that quiet is not the low-flying of one from the first drowsy by choice, and needing the prick of some strong passion or worldly ambition, to stimulate him into all the energy of which he is capable ; but rather the reaction of nature, after an escape from fate, dark and insane as in old Greek tragedy, following upon which the sense of mere relief becomes a kind of passion, as with one who, having narrowly escaped earthquake or shipwreck, finds a thing for grateful tears in just sitting quiet at home, under the wall, till the end of days.

He felt the genius of places ; and I sometimes think he resembles the places he knew and liked best, and where his lot fell—London, sixty-five years ago, with Covent Garden and the old theatres, and the Temple gardens still unspoiled, Thames gliding down, and beyond to north and south the fields at Enfield or Hampton, to which, " with their living trees," the thoughts wander " from the hard wood of the desk "— fields fresher, and coming nearer to town then, but in one of which the present writer re- members, on a brooding early summer's day, to have heard the cuckoo for the first time. Here, the surface of things is certainly humdrum, the streets dingy, the green places, where the child goes a-maying, tame enough. But nowhere are things more apt to respond to the brighter weather, nowhere is there so much difference between rain and sunshine, nowhere do the

CHARLES LAMB

clouds roll together more grandly ; those quaint
suburban pastorals gathering a certain quality of
grandeur from the background of the great city,
with its weighty atmosphere, and portent of
storm in the rapid light on dome and bleached
stone steeples.

1878.

SIR THOMAS BROWNE

ENGLISH prose literature towards the end of the seventeenth century, in the hands of Dryden and Locke, was becoming, as that of France had become at an earlier date, a matter of design and skilled practice, highly conscious of itself as an art, and, above all, correct. Up to that time it had been, on the whole, singularly informal and unprofessional, and by no means the literature of the "man of letters," as we understand him. Certain great instances there had been of literary structure or architecture—*The Ecclesiastical Polity*, *The Leviathan*—but for the most part that earlier prose literature is eminently occasional, closely determined by the eager practical aims of contemporary politics and theology, or else due to a man's own native instinct to speak because he cannot help speaking. Hardly aware of the habit, he likes talking to himself; and when he writes (still in undress) he does but take the "friendly reader" into his confidence. The type of this literature, obviously, is not Locke or Gibbon, but, above all others, Sir Thomas

Browne ; as Jean Paul is a good instance of it in German literature, always in its developments so much later than the English ; and as the best instance of it in French literature, in the century preceding Browne, is Montaigne, from whom indeed, in a great measure, all those tentative writers, or essayists, derive.

It was a result, perhaps, of the individualism and liberty of personal development, which, even for a Roman Catholic, were effects of the Reformation, that there was so much in Montaigne of the " subjective," as people say, of the singularities of personal character. Browne, too, bookish as he really is claims to give his readers a matter, " not picked from the leaves of any author, but bred amongst the weeds and tares " of his own brain. The faults of such literature are what we all recognise in it : unevenness, alike in thought and style ; lack of design ; and caprice—the lack of authority ; after the full play of which, there is so much to refresh one in the reasonable transparency of Hooker, representing thus early the tradition of a classical clearness in English literature, anticipated by Latimer and More, and to be fulfilled afterwards in Butler and Hume. But then, in recompense for that looseness and whim, in Sir Thomas Browne for instance, we have in those " quaint " writers, as they themselves understood the term (*coint*, adorned, but adorned with all the curious ornaments of their own predilection, provincial or archaic, certainly unfamiliar, and selected without reference to the taste or usages of other people) the charm of an absolute sincerity, with all the ingenuous and racy effect of what is circumstantial and peculiar in their growth.

> The whole creation is a mystery and particularly that of man. At the blast of His mouth were the rest of the creatures made, and at His bare word they started out of nothing. But in the frame of man He played the sensible operator, and seemed not so much to *create* as to *make* him. When He had separated the materials of other creatures, there consequently resulted a form and soul: but having raised the walls of man, He was driven to a second and harder creation—of a substance like Himself, an incorruptible and immortal soul.

There, we have the manner of Sir Thomas Browne, in exact expression of his mind!—minute and curious in its thinking, but with an effect, on the sudden, of a real sublimity or depth. His style is certainly an unequal one. It has the monumental aim which charmed, and perhaps influenced, Johnson—a dignity that can be attained only in such mental calm as follows long and learned pondering on the high subjects Browne loves to deal with. It has its garrulity, its various levels of painstaking, its mannerism, pleasant of its kind or tolerable, together with much, to us intolerable, but of which he was capable on a lazy summer afternoon down at Norwich. And all is so oddly mixed, showing, in its entire ignorance of self, how much he, and the sort of literature he represents, really stood in need of *technique,* of a formed taste in literature, of a literary architecture.

And yet perhaps we could hardly wish the result different, in him, any more than in the books of Burton and Fuller, or some other similar writers of that age—mental abodes, we might liken, after their own manner, to the little old private houses of some historic town grouped about its grand public structures, which, when they have survived at all, posterity is loth to part with. For, in their absolute sincerity, not only do these authors clearly exhibit themselves ("the unique peculiarity of the writer's mind," being, as Johnson says of Browne, "faithfully reflected in the form and matter of his work") but, even more than mere professionally instructed writers, they belong to, and reflect, the age they lived in. In essentials, of course, even Browne is by no means so unique among his contemporaries, and so singular, as he looks. And then, as the very condition of their work, there is an entire absence of personal restraint in dealing with the public, whose humours they come at last in a great measure to reproduce. To speak more properly, they have no sense of a "public" to deal with, at all—only a full confidence in the "friendly reader," as they love to call him. Hence their amazing pleasantry, their indulgence in their own conceits ; but hence also those unpremeditated wildflowers of speech we should

never have the good luck to find in any more
formal kind of literature.

It is, in truth, to the literary purpose of the
humourist, in the old-fashioned sense of the
term, that this method of writing naturally
allies itself—of the humourist to whom all
the world is but a spectacle in which nothing
is really alien from himself, who has hardly a
sense of the distinction between great and little
among things that are at all, and whose half-
pitying, half-amused sympathy is called out
especially by the seemingly small interests and
traits of character in the things or the people
around him. Certainly, in an age stirred by
great causes, like the age of Browne in England,
of Montaigne in France, that is not a type to
which one would wish to reduce all men of
letters. Still, in an age apt also to become
severe, or even cruel (its eager interest in those
great causes turning sour on occasion) the character of the humourist may well find its proper
influence, through that serene power, and the
leisure it has for conceiving second thoughts,
on the tendencies, conscious or unconscious, or
the fierce wills around it. Something of such a
humourist was Browne—not callous to men and
their fortunes; certainly not without opinions
of his own about them; and yet, undisturbed
by the civil war, by the fall, and then the
restoration, of the monarchy, through that
long quiet life (ending at last on the day

himself had predicted, as if at the moment
he had willed) in which "all existence," as
he says, "had been but food for contemplation."

Johnson, in beginning his *Life of Browne*,
remarks that Browne "seems to have had the
fortune, common among men of letters, of
raising little curiosity after their private life."
Whether or not, with the example of Johnson
himself before us, we can think just that, it is
certain that Browne's works are of a kind to
directly stimulate curiosity about himself—about
himself, as being manifestly so large a part of
those works ; and as a matter of fact we know
a great deal about his life, uneventful as in truth
it was. To himself, indeed, his life at Norwich,
as he gives us to understand, seemed wonderful
enough. "Of these wonders," says Johnson,
"the view that can now be taken of his life
offers no appearance." But "we carry with
us," as Browne writes, "the wonders we seek
without us," and we may note on the other
hand, a circumstance which his daughter,
Mrs. Lyttleton, tells us of his childhood :
"His father used to open his breast when he
was asleep, and kiss it in prayers over him, as
'tis said of Origen's father, that the Holy Ghost
would take possession there." It was perhaps
because the son inherited an aptitude for a
like profound kindling of sentiment in the
taking of his life, that, uneventful as it was,

commonplace as it seemed to Johnson, to Browne himself it was so full of wonders, and so stimulates the curiosity of his more careful reader of to-day. "What influence," says Johnson again, "learning has had on its possessors may be doubtful." Well! the influence of his great learning, of his constant research on Browne, was its imaginative influence—that it completed his outfit as a poetic visionary, stirring all the strange "conceit" of his nature to its depths.

Browne himself dwells, in connexion with the first publication (extorted by circumstance) of the *Religio Medici*, on the natural "inactivity of his disposition"; and he does, as I have said, pass very quietly through an exciting time. Born in the year of the Gunpowder Plot, he was not, in truth, one of those clear and clarifying souls which, in an age alike of practical and mental confusion, can anticipate and lay down the bases of reconstruction, like Bacon or Hooker. His mind has much of the perplexity which was part of the atmosphere of the time. Not that he is without his own definite opinions on events. For him, Cromwell is a usurper, the death of Charles an abominable murder. In spite of what is but an affectation, perhaps, of the sceptical mood, he is a Churchman too; one of those who entered fully into the Anglican position, so full of sympathy with those ceremonies and observances which "misguided zeal terms superstition," that there were some Roman Catholics who thought that nothing but custom and education kept him from their communion. At the Restoration he rejoices to see the return of the comely Anglican order in old episcopal Norwich, with its ancient churches ; the antiquity, in particular, of the English Church being, characteristically, one of the things he most valued in it, vindicating it, when occasion came, against the "unjust scandal" of those who made that Church a creation of Henry the Eighth. As to Romanists—he makes no scruple to "enter their churches in defect of ours." He cannot laugh at, but rather pities, "the fruitless journeys of pilgrims—for there is something in it of devotion." He could never "hear the *Ave Mary !* bell without an *oraison.*" At a solemn procession he has "wept abundantly." How English, in truth, all this really is ! It reminds one how some of the most popular of English writers, in many a half-conscious expression, have witnessed to a susceptibility in the English mind itself, in spite of the Reformation, to what is affecting in religious ceremony. Only, in religion as in politics, Browne had no turn for disputes ; was suspicious of them, indeed ; knowing, as he says with true acumen, that "a man may be in as just possession of truth as of a city, and yet be forced to surrender," even in controversies not necessarily maladroit—an image in which we may trace a little contemporary colouring.

The *Enquiries into Vulgar Errors* appeared in the year 1646 ; a year which found him very hard on " the vulgar." His suspicion, in the abstract, of what Bacon calls *Idola Fori*, the Idols of the Market-place, takes a special emphasis from the course of events about him :—" being erroneous in their single numbers, once huddled together, they will be error itself." And yet, congruously with a dreamy sweetness of character we may find expressed in his very features, he seems not greatly concerned at the temporary suppression of the institutions he values so much. He seems to possess some inward Platonic reality of them—church or monarchy—to hold by in idea, quite beyond the reach of Roundhead or unworthy Cavalier. In the power of what is inward and inviolable in his religion, he can still take note : " In my solitary and retired imagination (*neque enim cum porticus aut me lectulus accepit, desum mihi*) I remember I am not alone, and therefore forget not to contemplate Him and His attributes who is ever with me."

His father, a merchant of London, with some claims to ancient descent, left him early in possession of ample means. Educated at Winchester and Oxford, he visited Ireland, France, and Italy ; and in the year 1633, at the age of twenty-eight, became Doctor of Medicine at Leyden. Three years later he established himself as a physician at Norwich for the remainder of his life, having married a lady, described as beautiful and attractive, and affectionate also, as we may judge from her letters and postscripts to those of her husband, in an orthography of a homeliness amazing even for that age. Dorothy Browne bore him ten children, six of whom he survived.

Their house at Norwich, even then an old one it would seem, must have grown, through long years of acquisition, into an odd cabinet of antiquities—antiquities properly so called ; his old Roman, or Romanised British urns, from Walsingham or Brampton, for instance, and those natural objects which he studied somewhat in the temper of a curiosity-hunter or antiquary. In one of the old churchyards of Norwich he makes the first discovery of *adipocere*, of which grim substance "a portion still remains with him." For his multifarious experiments he must have had his laboratory. The old window-stanchions had become magnetic, proving, as he thinks, that iron "acquires verticity" from long lying in one position. Once we find him re-tiling the place. It was then, perhaps, that he made the observation that bricks and tiles also acquire "magnetic alliciency"—one's whole house, one might fancy ; as indeed, he holds the earth itself to be a vast lodestone.

The very faults of his literary work, its desultoriness, the time it costs his readers, that

slow Latinity which Johnson imitated from him,
those lengthy leisurely terminations which busy
posterity will abbreviate, all breathe of the long
quiet of the place. Yet he is by no means
indolent. Besides wide book-learning, experimental research at home, and indefatigable
observation in the open air, he prosecutes the
ordinary duties of a physician ; contrasting himself indeed with other students, "whose quiet
and unmolested doors afford no such distractions." To most persons of mind sensitive as
his, his chosen studies would have seemed full of
melancholy, turning always, as they did, upon
death and decay. It is well, perhaps, that life
should be something of a "meditation upon
death" : but to many, certainly, Browne's would
have seemed too like a lifelong following of
one's own funeral. A museum is seldom a
cheerful place—oftenest induces the feeling that
nothing could ever have been young ; and to
Browne the whole world is a museum ; all the
grace and beauty it has being of a somewhat
mortified kind. Only, for him (poetic dream, or
philosophic apprehension, it was this which
never failed to evoke his wonderful genius for
exquisitely impassioned speech) over all those
ugly anatomical preparations, as though over
miraculous saintly relics, there was the perpetual
flicker of a surviving spiritual ardency, one day
to reassert itself—stranger far than any fancied
odylic gravelights !

SIR THOMAS BROWNE

When Browne settled at Norwich, being then about thirty-six years old, he had already completed the *Religio Medici*; a desultory collection of observations designed for himself only and a few friends, at all events with no purpose of immediate publication. It had been lying by him for seven years, circulating privately in his own extraordinarily perplexed manuscript, or in manuscript copies, when, in 1642, an incorrect printed version from one of those copies, "much corrupted by transcription at various hands," appeared anonymously. Browne, decided royalist as he was in spite of seeming indifference, connects this circumstance with the unscrupulous use of the press for political purposes, and especially against the king, at that time. Just here a romantic figure comes on the scene. Son of the unfortunate young Everard Digby who perished on the scaffold for some half-hearted participation in the Gunpowder Plot, Kenelm Digby, brought up in the reformed religion, had returned in manhood to the religion of his father. In his intellectual composition he had, in common with Browne, a scientific interest, oddly tinged with both poetry and scepticism : he had also a strong sympathy with religious reaction, and a more than sentimental love for a seemingly vanishing age of faith, which he, for one, would not think of as vanishing. A copy of that surreptitious edition of the *Religio Medici* found him a prisoner on suspicion of a too active royalism, and with much time on his hands. The Roman Catholic, although, secure in his definite orthodoxy, he finds himself indifferent on many points (on the reality of witchcraft, for instance) concerning which Browne's more timid, personally grounded faith might indulge no scepticism, forced himself, nevertheless, to detect a vein of rationalism in a book which on the whole much attracted him, and hastily put forth his "animadversions" upon it. Browne, with all his distaste for controversy, thus found himself committed to a dispute, and his reply came with the correct edition of the *Religio Medici* published at last with his name. There have been many efforts to formulate the "religion of the layman," which might be rightly understood, perhaps, as something more than what is called "natural," yet less than ecclesiastical, or "professional" religion. Though its habitual mode of conceiving experience is on a different plane, yet it would recognise the legitimacy of the traditional religious interpretation of that experience, generally and by implication ; only, with a marked reserve as to religious particulars, both of thought and language, out of a real reverence or awe, as proper only for a special place. Such is the lay religion, as we may find it in Addison, in Gray, in Thackeray ; and there is something of a concession—a concession, on second thoughts—about it. Browne's *Religio Medici* is designed as the expression of a mind

more difficult of belief than that of the mere
" layman," as above described ; it is meant for
the religion of the man of science. Actually, it
is something less to the point, in any balancing
of the religious against the worldly view of
things, than the religion of the layman, as just
now defined. For Browne, in spite of his pro-
fession of boisterous doubt, has no real difficulties, and his religion, certainly, nothing of the
character of a concession. He holds that there
has never existed an atheist. Not that he is
credulous ; but that his religion is only the correlative of himself, his peculiar character and
education, a religion of manifold association.
For him, the wonders of religion, its supernatural events or agencies, are almost natural
facts or processes. " Even in this material
fabric, the spirits walk as freely exempt from
the affection of time, place and motion, as
beyond the extremest circumference." Had not
Divine interference designed to raise the dead,
nature herself is in act to do it—to lead out the
" incinerated " soul from the retreats of her dark
laboratory. Certainly Browne has not, like
Pascal, made the " great resolution," by the
apprehension that it is just in the contrast of the
moral world to the world with which science
deals that religion finds its proper basis. It is
from the homelessness of the world which science
analyses so victoriously, its dark unspirituality,
wherein the soul he is conscious of seems such a

stranger, that Pascal "turns again to his rest," in the conception of a world of wholly reasonable and moral agencies. For Browne, on the contrary, the light is full, design everywhere obvious, its conclusion easy to draw, all small and great things marked clearly with the signature of the "Word." The adhesion, the difficult adhesion, of men such as Pascal, is an immense contribution to religious controversy ; the concession, again, of a man like Addison, of great significance there. But in the adhesion of Browne, in spite of his crusade against "vulgar errors," there is no real significance. The *Religio Medici* is a contribution, not to faith, but to piety ; a refinement and correction, such as piety often stands in need of ; a help, not so much to religious belief in a world of doubt, as to the maintenance of the religious mood amid the interests of a secular calling.

From about this time Browne's letters afford a pretty clear view of his life as it passed in the house at Norwich. Many of these letters represent him in correspondence with the singular men who shared his own half poetic, half scientific turn of mind, with that impressibility towards what one might call the thaumaturgic elements in nature which has often made men dupes, and which is certainly an element in the somewhat atrabiliar mental complexion of that age in England. He corresponds seriously with William Lily, the astrologer ; is acquainted

with Dr. Dee, who had some connexion with
Norwich, and has " often heard him affirm,
sometimes with oaths, that he had seen trans-
mutation of pewter dishes and flagons into silver
(at least) which the goldsmiths at Prague bought
of him." Browne is certainly an honest investigator ; but it is still with a faint hope of
something like that upon fitting occasion, and
on the alert always for surprises in nature (as if
nature had a rhetoric, at times, to deliver to us,
like those sudden and surprising flowers of his
own poctic style) that he listens to her everyday
talk so attentively. Of strange animals, strange
cures, and the like, his correspondence is full.
The very errors he combats are, of course, the
curiosities of error—those fascinating, irresistible,
popular, errors, which various kinds of people
have insisted on gliding into because they like
them. Even his heresies were old oncs—the
very fossils of capricious opinion.

It is as an industrious local naturalist that
Browne comes before us first, full of the fantastic
minute life in the fens and " Broads " around
Norwich, its various sea and marsh birds. He is
something of a vivisectionist also, and we may
not be surprised at it, perhaps, in an age which,
for the propagation of truth, was ready to cut off
men's ears. He finds one day " a *Scarabæus
capricornus odoratus,*" which he takes " to be
mentioned by Monfetus, folio 150. He saith,
' *Nucem moschatam et cinnamomum vere spirat*'—

but to me it smelt like roses, santalum, and ambergris." " *Musca tuliparum moschata*," again, " is a small bee-like fly of an excellent fragrant odour, which I have often found at the bottom of the flowers of tulips." Is this within the experience of modern entomologists ?

The *Garden of Cyrus*, though it ends indeed with a passage of wonderful felicity, certainly emphasises (to say the least) the defects of Browne's literary good qualities. His chimeric fancy carries him here into a kind of frivolousness, as if he felt almost too safe with his public, and were himself not quite serious, or dealing fairly with it ; and in a writer such as Browne levity must of necessity be a little ponderous. Still, like one of those stiff gardens, half-way between the medieval garden and the true "English " garden of Temple or Walpole, actually to be seen in the background of some of the conventional portraits of that day, the fantasies of this indescribable exposition of the mysteries of the *quincunx* form part of the complete portrait of Browne himself ; and it is in connexion with it that, once or twice, the quaintly delightful pen of Evelyn comes into the correspondence—in connexion with the " hortulane pleasure." " Norwich," he writes to Browne, "is a place, I understand, much addicted to the flowery part." Professing himself a believer in the operation " of the air and genius of gardens upon human spirits, towards virtue and sanctity," he is all for

SIR THOMAS BROWNE

natural gardens as against "those which appear
like gardens of paste-board and march-pane, and
smell more of paint than of flowers and verdure."
Browne is in communication also with Ashmole
and Dugdale, the famous antiquaries; to the
latter of whom, who had written a work on
the history of the embanking of fens, he communicates the discovery of certain coins, on a
piece of ground "in the nature of an island in
the fens."

Far more interesting certainly than those
curious scientific letters is Browne's "domestic
correspondence." Dobson, Charles the First's
" English Tintoret," would seem to have painted
a life-sized picture of Sir Thomas Browne and
his family, after the manner of those big, urbane,
family groups, then coming into fashion with
the Dutch Masters. Of such a portrait nothing
is now known. But in these old-fashioned,
affectionate letters, transmitted often, in those
troublous times, with so much difficulty, we
have what is almost as graphic—a numerous
group, in which, although so many of Browne's
children died young, he was happy; with
Dorothy Browne, occasionally adding her charming, ill-spelt postscripts to her husband's letters;
the religious daughter who goes to daily prayers
after the Restoration, which brought Browne
the honour of knighthood; and, above all, two
Toms, son and grandson of Sir Thomas, the
latter being the son of Dr. Edward Browne,

now become distinguished as a physician in London (he attended John, Earl of Rochester, in his last illness at Woodstock) and his childish existence as he lives away from his proper home in London, in the old house at Norwich, two hundred years ago, we see like a thing of to-day.

At first the two brothers, Edward and Thomas (the elder) are together in everything. Then Edward goes abroad for his studies, and Thomas, quite early, into the navy, where he certainly develops into a wonderfully gallant figure ; passing away, however, from the correspondence, it is uncertain how, before he was of full age. From the first he is understood to be a lad of parts. " If you practise to write, you will have a good pen and style : " and a delightful, boyish journal of his remains, describing a tour the two brothers made in September 1662 among the Derbyshire hills. " I received your two last letters," he writes to his father from aboard the *Marie Rose*, " and give you many thanks for the discourse you sent me out of Vossius : *De motu marium et ventorum.* It seemed very hard to me at first ; but I have now beaten it, and I wish I had the book." His father is pleased to think that he is " like to proceed not only a good navigator, but a good scholar " : and he finds the much exacting, old classical prescription for the character of the brave man fulfilled in him. On 16th July 1666 the young man writes —still from the *Marie Rose*—

SIR THOMAS BROWNE

If it were possible to get an opportunity to send as often as I am desirous to write, you should hear more often from me, being now so near the grand action, from which I would by no means be absent. I extremely long for that thundering day : wherein I hope you shall hear we have behaved ourselves like men, and to the honour of our country. I thank you for your directions for my ears against the noise of the guns, but I have found that I could endure it ; nor is it so intolerable as most conceive ; especially when men are earnest, and intent upon their business, unto whom muskets sound but like pop-guns. It is impossible to express unto another how a smart sea-fight elevates the spirits of a man, and makes him depise all dangers. In and after all sea-fights, I have been very thirsty.

He died, as I said, early in life. We only hear of him later in connexion with a trait of character observed in Tom the grandson, whose winning ways, and tricks of bodily and mental growth, are duly recorded in these letters : the reader will, I hope, pardon the following extracts from them :—

Little Tom is lively. . . . Frank is fayne sometimes to play him asleep with a fiddle. When we send away our letters he scribbles a paper and will have it sent to his sister, and saith she doth not know how many fine things there are in Norwich. . . . He delights his grandfather when he comes home.

Tom gives you many thanks for his clothes (from London). He has appeared very fine this King's day with them.

Tom presents his duty. A gentleman at our election asked Tom who hee was for ? and he answered, " For all four." The gentleman replied that he answered like a physician's son.

Tom would have his grandmother, his aunt Betty, and Frank, valentines : but hee conditioned with them that they should give him nothing of any kind that hee had ever had or seen before.

APPRECIATIONS

" Tom is just now gone to see two bears which are to be shown." "Tom, his duty. He is begging books and reading of them." "The players are at the Red Lion hard by ; and Tom goes sometimes to see a play."

And then one day he stirs old memories—

The fairings were welcome to Tom. He finds about the house divers things that were your brother's (the late Edward's), and Betty sometimes tells him stories about him, so that he was importunate with her to write his life in a quarter of a sheet of paper, and read it unto him, and will have still some more added.

Just as I am writing (learnedly about a comet, 7th January 1680-81) Tom comes and tells me the blazing star is in the yard, and calls me to see it. It was but dim, and the sky not clear. . . . I am very sensible of this sharp weather.

He seems to have come to no good end, riding forth one stormy night. *Requiescat in pace !*
Of this long, leisurely existence the chief events were Browne's rare literary publications ; some of his writings indeed having been left unprinted till after his death ; while in the circumstances of the issue of every one of them there is something accidental, as if the world might have missed it altogether. Even the *Discourse of Vulgar Errors*, the longest and most elaborate of his works, is entirely discursive and occasional, coming to an end with no natural conclusion, but only because the writer chose to leave off just there ; and few probably have been the readers of the book as a consecutive whole. At times indeed we seem to have in it observations only, or notes, preliminary to some more orderly composition. Dip into it : read, for

instance, the chapter " Of the Ring-finger," or the chapters " Of the Long Life of the Deer," and on the "Pictures of Mermaids, Unicorns, and some Others," and the part will certainly seem more than the whole. Try to read it through, and you will soon feel cloyed ;—miss very likely, its real worth to the fancy, the literary fancy (which finds its pleasure in inventive word and phrase) and become dull to the really vivid beauties of a book so lengthy, but with no real evolution. Though there are words, phrases, constructions innumerable, which remind one how much the work initiated in France by Madame de Rambouillet—work, done for England, we may think perhaps imperfectly, in the next century by Johnson and others—was really needed ; yet the capacities of Browne's manner of writing, coming as it did so directly from the man, are felt even in his treatment of matters of science. As with Buffon, his full, ardent, sympathetic vocabulary, the poetry of his language, a poetry inherent in its elementary particles—the word, the epithet— helps to keep his eye, and the eye of the reader, on the object before it, and conduces directly to the purpose of the naturalist, the observer.

But, only one half observation, its other half consisting of very out-of-the-way book-lore, this work displays Browne still in the character of the antiquary, as that age understood him. He is a kind of Elias Ashmole, but dealing with natural objects ; which are for him, in the first

place, and apart from the remote religious hints
and intimations they carry with them, curiosities.
He seems to have no true sense of natural law, as
Bacon understood it ; nor even of that immanent
reason in the natural world, which the Platonic
tradition supposes. "Things are really true," he
says, "as they correspond unto God's conception ;
and have so much verity as they hold of conformity unto that intellect, in whose idea they had
their first determinations." But, actually, what
he is busy in the record of, are matters more or
less of the nature of caprices ; as if things, after
all, were significant of their higher verity only at
random, and in a sort of surprises, like music in
old instruments suddenly touched into sound by
a wandering finger, among the lumber of people's
houses. Nature, "the art of God," as he says,
varying a little a phrase used also by Hobbes, in
a work printed later—Nature, he seems to protest, is only a little less magical, its processes
only a little less in the way of alchemy, than you
had supposed. We feel that, as with that disturbed age in England generally (and it is here
that he, with it, is so interesting, curious, old-
world, and unlike ourselves) his supposed experience might at any moment be broken in upon
by a hundred forms of a natural magic, only not
quite so marvellous as that older sort of magic, or
alchmy, he is at so much pains to expose ; and
the large promises of which, its large words too,
he still regretfully enjoys.

SIR THOMAS BROWNE

And yet the *Discourse of Vulgar Errors*, seeming, as it often does, to be a serious refutation of fairy tales—arguing, for instance, against the literal truth of the poetic statement that "The pigeon hath no gall," and such questions as " Whether men weigh heavier dead than alive ? " being characteristic questions—is designed, with much ambition, under its pedantic Greek title *Pseudodoxia Epidemica*, as a criticism, a cathartic, an instrument for the clarifying of the intellect. He begins from "that first error in Paradise," wondering much at "man's deceivability in his perfection,"—"at such gross deceit." He enters in this connexion, with a kind of poetry of scholasticism which may interest the student of *Paradise Lost*, into what we may call the intellectual and moral by-play of the situation of the first man and woman in Paradise, with strange queries about it. Did Adam, for instance, already know of the fall of the Angels ? Did he really believe in death, till Abel died ? It is from Julius Scaliger that he takes his motto, to the effect that the true knowledge of things must be had from things themselves, not from books ; and he seems as seriously concerned as Bacon to dissipate the crude impressions of a false "common sense," of false science, and a fictitious authority. Inverting, oddly, Plato's theory that all learning is but reminiscence, he reflects with a sigh how much of oblivion must needs be involved in the getting of any true knowledge. " Men that adore times past, consider not that those times were once present (that is, as our own are) and ourselves unto those to come, as they unto us at present." That, surely, coming from one both by temperament and habit so great an antiquary, has the touch of something like an influence in the atmosphere of the time. That there was any actual connexion between Browne's work and Bacon's is but a surmise. Yet we almost seem to hear Bacon when Browne discourses on the " use of doubts, and the advantages which might be derived from drawing up a calendar of doubts, falsehoods, and popular errors ; " and, as from Bacon, one gets the impression that men really have been very much the prisoners of their own crude or pedantic terms, notions, associations; that they have been very indolent in testing very simple matters—with a wonderful kind of "supinity," as he calls it. In Browne's chapter on the " Sources of Error," again, we may trace much resemblance to Bacon's striking doctrine of the *Idola*, the " shams " men fall down and worship. Taking source respectively, from the " common infirmity of human nature," from the " erroneous disposition of the people," from " confident adherence to authority," the errors which Browne chooses to deal with may be registered as identical with Bacon's *Idola Tribus*, *Fori*, *Theatri;* the idols of our common human nature ; of the vulgar, when they get together ; and of the learned, when they get together.

SIR THOMAS BROWNE

But of the fourth species of error noted by Bacon, the *Idola Specus*, the Idols of the Cave, that whole tribe of illusions, which are "bred amongst the weeds and tares of one's own brain," Browne tells us nothing by way of criticism ; was himself, rather, a lively example of their operation. Throw those illusions, those "idols," into concrete or personal form, suppose them introduced among the other forces of an active intellect, and you have Sir Thomas Browne himself. The sceptical inquirer who rises from his cathartic, his purging of error, a believer in the supernatural character of pagan oracles, and a cruel judge of supposed witches, must still need as much as ever that elementary conception of the right method and the just limitations of knowledge, by power of which he should not just strain out a single error here or there, but make a final precipitate of fallacy.

And yet if the temperament had been deducted from Browne's work—that inherent and strongly marked way of deciding things, which has guided with so surprising effect the musings of the *Letter to a Friend*, and the *Urn-Burial*—we should probably have remembered him little. Pity ! some may think, for himself at least, that he had not lived earlier, and still believed in the mandrake, for instance ; its fondness for places of execution, and its human cries "on eradication, with hazard of life to them that pull it up." "In philosophy," he observes, meaning to contrast his free-thinking in that department with his orthodoxy in religion—in philosophy, "where truth seems double-faced, there is no man more paradoxical than myself:" which is true, we may think, in a further sense than he meant, and that it was the "paradoxical" that he actually preferred. Happy, at all events, he still remained —undisturbed and happy—in a hundred native prepossessions, some certainly valueless, some of them perhaps invaluable. And while one feels that no real logic of fallacies has been achieved by him, one feels still more how little the construction of that branch of logical inquiry really helps men's minds ; fallacy, like truth itself, being a matter so dependent on innate gift of apprehension, so extra-logical and personal ; the original perception counting for almost everything, the mere inference for so little ! Yes ! " A man may be in as just possession of truth as of a city, and yet be forced to surrender," even in controversies not necessarily maladroit.

The really stirring poetry of science is not in guesses, or facile divinations about it, but in its larger ascertained truths—the order of infinite space, the slow method and vast results of infinite time. For Browne, however, the sense of poetry which so overmasters his scientific procedure, depends chiefly on its vaguer possibilities ; the empirical philosophy, even after Bacon, being still dominated by a temper, resultant from the general unsettlement of men's minds at the Reformation, which may be summed up in the famous question of Montaigne —*Que sçais-je?* The cold-blooded method of observation and experiment was creeping but slowly over the domain of science ; and such unreclaimed portions of it as the phenomena of magnetism had an immense fascination for men like Browne and Digby. Here, in those parts of natural philosophy "but yet in discovery," "the America and untravelled parts of truth," lay for them the true prospect of science, like the new world itself to a geographical discoverer such as Raleigh. And welcome as one of the minute hints of that country far ahead of them, the strange bird, or floating fragment of unfamiliar vegetation, which met those early navigators, there was a certain fantastic experiment, in which, as was alleged, Paracelsus had been lucky. For Browne and others it became the crucial type of the kind of agency in nature which, as they conceived, it was the proper function of science to reveal in larger operation. "The subject of my last letter," says Dr. Henry Power, then a student, writing to Browne in 1648, the last year of Charles the First, "being so high and noble a piece of chemistry, invites me once more to request an experimental eviction of it from yourself; and I hope you will not chide my importunity in this petition, or be angry at my so frequent knockings at your door to obtain a grant of so great and admirable a mystery." What the enthusiastic young student expected from Browne, so high and noble a piece of chemistry, was the " re-individualling of an incinerated plant"—a violet, turning to freshness, and smelling sweet again, out of its ashes, under some genially fitted conditions of the chemic art.

Palingenesis, resurrection, effected by orderly prescription—the " re-individualling" of an " incinerated organism "—is a subject which affords us a natural transition to the little book of the *Hydriotaphia*, or *Treatise of Urn-Burial*— about fifty or sixty pages—which, together with a very singular letter not printed till after Browne's death, is perhaps, after all, the best justification of Browne's literary reputation, as it were his own curiously figured urn, and treasure-place of immortal memory.

In its first presentation to the public this letter was connected with Browne's *Christian Morals;* but its proper and sympathetic collocation would be rather with the *Urn-Burial*, of which it is a kind of prelude, or strikes the keynote. He is writing in a very complex situation—to a friend, upon occasion of the death of a common friend. The deceased apparently had been little known to Browne himself till his recent visits, while the intimate friend to whom he is writing had been absent at the time ; and the leading motive of Browne's letter is the deep impression he has received during those visits, of a sort of physical beauty in the coming of death, with which he still surprises and moves his reader. There had been, in this case, a tardiness and reluctancy in the circumstances of dissolution, which had permitted him, in the character of a physician, as it were to assist at the spiritualising of the bodily frame by natural process; a wonderful new type of a kind of mortified grace being evolved by the way. The spiritual body had anticipated the formal moment of death; the alert soul, in that tardy decay, changing its vesture gradually, and as if piece by piece. The infinite future had invaded this life perceptibly to the senses, like the ocean felt far inland up a tidal river. Nowhere, perhaps, is the attitude of questioning awe on the threshold of another life displayed with the expressiveness of this unique morsel of literature; though there is something of the same kind, in another than the literary medium, in the delicate monumental sculpture of the early Tuscan School, as also in many of the designs of William Blake, often, though unconsciously, much in sympathy with those unsophisticated Italian workmen. With him, as with them, and with the writer of the *Letter to a Friend upon the occasion of the death of his intimate Friend,*—so strangely! the visible function of death is but to refine, to detach from aught that is vulgar. And this elfin letter, really an impromptu epistle to a friend, affords the best possible light on the general temper of the man

who could be moved by the accidental discovery
of those old urns at Walsingham—funeral relics
of "Romans, or Britons Romanised which had
learned Roman customs"—to the composition
of that wonderful book the *Hydriotaphia*. He
had drawn up a short account of the circumstance
at the moment; but it was after ten years'
brooding that he put forth the finished treatise,
dedicated to an eminent collector of ancient coins
and other rarities, with congratulations that he
"can daily command the view of so many
imperial faces," and (by way of frontispiece) with
one of the urns, "drawn with a coal taken out
of it and found among the burnt bones." The
discovery had resuscitated for him a whole world
of latent observation, from life, from out-of-the-
way reading, from the natural world, and fused
into a composition, which with all its quaintness
we may well pronounce classical, all the hetero-
geneous elements of that singular mind. The
desire to "record these risen ashes and not to let
them be buried twice among us," had set free,
in his manner of conceiving things, something
not wholly analysable, something that may be
properly called genius, which shapes his use of
common words to stronger and deeper senses, in
a way unusual in prose writing. Let the reader,
for instance, trace his peculiarly sensitive use of
the epithets *thin* and *dark*, both here and in the
Letter to a Friend.

Upon what a grand note he can begin and end

chapter or paragraph !—" When the funeral pyre
was out, and the last valediction over : "—" And
a large part of the earth is still in the urn unto
us." Dealing with a very vague range of feelings, it is his skill to associate them to very
definite objects. Like the Soul, in Blake's design,
" exploring the recesses of the tomb," he carries
a light, the light of the poetic faith which he
cannot put off him, into those dark places, " the
abode of worms and pismires," peering round
with a boundless curiosity and no fear ; noting
the various casuistical considerations of men's
last form of self-love ; all those whims of humanity as a " student of perpetuity," the mortuary
customs of all nations, which, from their very
closeness to our human nature, arouse in most
minds only a strong feeling of distaste. There
is something congruous with the impassive piety
of the man in his waiting on accident from
without to take start for the work, which, of all
his work, is most truly touched by the " divine
spark." Delightsome as its eloquence is actually
found to be, that eloquence is attained out of
a certain difficulty and halting crabbedness of
expression ; the wretched punctuation of the
piece being not the only cause of its impressing
the reader with the notion that he is but dealing
with a collection of notes for a more finished
composition, and of a different kind ; perhaps
a purely erudite treatise on its subject, with
detachment of all personal colour now adhering

to it. Out of an atmosphere of all-pervading
oddity and quaintness—the quaintness of mind
which reflects that this disclosing of the urns of
the ancients hath " left unto our view some parts
which they never beheld themselves "—arises a
work really ample and grand, nay ! classical, as I
said, by virtue of the effectiveness with which it
fixes a type in literature ; as, indeed, at its best,
romantic literature (and Browne is genuinely
romantic) in every period attains classical quality,
giving true measure of the very limited value of
those well-worn critical distinctions. And though
the *Urn-Burial* certainly has much of the character of a poem, yet one is never allowed to
forget that it was designed, candidly, as a
scientific treatise on one department of ancient
" culture " (as much so as Guichard's curious old
French book on *Divers Manners of Burial*) and
was the fruit of much labour, in the way
especially of industrious selection from remote
and difficult writers ; there being then few or no
handbooks, or anything like our modern short-
cuts to varied knowledge. Quite unaffectedly, a
curious learning saturates, with a kind of grey
and aged colour most apt and congruous with the
subject-matter, all the thoughts that arise in him.
His great store of reading, so freely displayed, he
uses almost as poetically as Milton ; like him,
profiting often by the mere sonorous effect of
some heroic or ancient name, which he can
adapt to that same sort of learned sweetness of

cadence with which so many of his single sentences are made to fall upon the ear.

Pope Gregory, that great religious poet, requested by certain eminent persons to send them some of those relics he sought for so devoutly in all the lurking-places of old Rome, took up, it is said, a portion of common earth, and delivered it to the messengers; and, on their expressing surprise at such a gift, pressed the earth together in his hand, whereupon the sacred blood of the Martyrs was beheld flowing out between his fingers. The veneration of relics became a part of Christian (as some may think it a part of natural) religion. All over Rome we may count how much devotion in fine art is owing to it; and, through all ugliness or superstition, its intention still speaks clearly to serious minds. The poor dead bones, ghastly and forbidding :— we know what Shakespeare would have felt about them.—"Beat not the bones of the buried: when he breathed, he was a man!" And it is with something of a similar feeling that Browne is full, on the common and general ground of humanity; an awe-stricken sympathy with those, whose bones "lie at the mercies of the living," strong enough to unite all his various chords of feeling into a single strain of impressive and genuine poetry. His real interest is in what may be called the curiosities of our common humanity. As another might be moved at the sight of Alexander's bones, or Saint Edmund's, or Saint Cecilia's,

so he is full of a fine poetical excitement at such
lowly relics as the earth hides almost everywhere
beneath our feet. But it is hardly fair to take our
leave amid these grievous images of so happy a
writer as Sir Thomas Browne ; so great a lover of
the open air, under which much of his life was
passed. His work, late one night, draws to a natural
close : — " To keep our eyes open longer," he
bethinks himself suddenly, " were but to act our
Antipodes. The huntsmen are up in America ! "

What a fund of open-air cheerfulness, there !
in turning to sleep. Still, even when we are
dealing with a writer in whom mere style
counts for so much as with Browne, it is impossible to ignore his matter ; and it is with
religion he is really occupied from first to last,
hardly less than Richard Hooker. And his
religion, too, after all, was a religion of cheerfulness : he has no great consciousness of evil in
things, and is no fighter. His religion, if one
may say so, was all profit to him ; among other
ways, in securing an absolute staidness and
placidity of temper, for the intellectual work
which was the proper business of his life. His
contributions to " evidence," in the *Religio
Medici*, for instance, hardly tell, because he
writes out of view of a really philosophical
criticism. What does tell in him, in this
direction, is the witness he brings to men's
instinct of survival—the " intimations of immortality," as Wordsworth terms them, which

were natural with him in surprising force.   As was said of Jean Paul, his special subject was the immortality of the soul ; with an assurance as personal, as fresh and original, as it was, on the one hand, in those old half-civilised people who had deposited the urns ; on the other hand, in the cynical French poet of the nineteenth century, who did not think, but knew, that *his* soul was imperishable.   He lived in an age in which that philosophy made a great stride which ends with Hume ; and his lesson, if we may be pardoned for taking away a " lesson " from so ethical a writer, is the force of men's temperaments in the management of opinion, their own or that of others ;—that it is not merely different degrees of bare intellectual power which cause men to approach in different degrees to this or that intellectual programme. Could he have foreseen the mature result of that mechanical analysis which Bacon had applied to nature, and Hobbes to the mind of man, there is no reason to think that he would have surrendered his own chosen hypothesis concerning them.   He represents, in an age, the intellectual powers of which tend strongly to agnosticism, that class of minds to which the supernatural view of things is still credible. The non-mechanical theory of nature has had its grave adherents since : to the non-mechanical theory of man — that he is in contact with a moral order on a different plane from the mechanical order—thousands, of the most various types and degrees of intellectual power, always adhere ; a fact worth the consideration of all ingenuous thinkers, if (as is certainly the case with colour, music, number, for instance) there may be whole regions of fact, the recognition of which belongs to one and not to another, which people may possess in various degrees ; for the knowledge of which, therefore, one person is dependent upon another ; and in relation to which the appropriate means of cognition must lie among the elements of what we call individual temperament, so that what looks like a pre-judgment may be really a legitimate apprehension. " Men are what they are," and are not wholly at the mercy of formal conclusions from their formally limited premises. Browne passes his whole life in observation and inquiry : he is a genuine investigator, with every opportunity : the mind of the age all around him seems passively yielding to an almost foregone intellectual result, to a philosophy of disillusion. But he thinks all that a prejudice ; and not from any want of intellectual power certainly, but from some inward consideration, some afterthought, from the antecedent gravitation of his own general character—or, will you say ? from that unprecipitated infusion of fallacy in him—he fails to draw, unlike almost all the rest of the world, the conclusion ready to hand.

1886.

"LOVE'S LABOURS LOST"

Love's Labours Lost is one of the earliest of Shakespeare's dramas, and has many of the peculiarities of his poems, which are also the work of his earlier life. The opening speech of the king on the immortality of fame — on the triumph of fame over death — and the nobler parts of Biron, display something of the monumental style of Shakespeare's Sonnets, and are not without their conceits of thought and expression. This connexion of *Love's Labours Lost* with Shakespeare's poems is further enforced by the actual insertion in it of three sonnets and a faultless song ; which, in accordance with his practice in other plays, are inwoven into the argument of the piece and, like the golden ornaments of a fair woman, give it a peculiar air of distinction. There is merriment in it also, with choice illustrations of both wit and humour ; a laughter, often exquisite, ringing, if faintly, yet as genuine laughter still, though sometimes sinking into mere burlesque, which has not lasted quite so well. And Shakespeare

brings a serious effect out of the trifling of his
characters.   A dainty love-making is inter-
changed with the more cumbrous play : below
the many artifices of Biron's amorous speeches
we may trace sometimes the " unutterable longing ; " and the lines in which Katherine describes
the blighting through love of her younger sister
are one of the most touching things in older
literature.[1]   Again, how many echoes seem
awakened by those strange words, actually said
in jest !—" The sweet war-man (Hector of Troy)
is dead and rotten ; sweet chucks, beat not the
bones of the buried : when he breathed, he was
a man ! "—words which may remind us of
Shakespeare's own epitaph.   In the last scene,
an ingenious turn is given to the action, so that
the piece does not conclude after the manner of
other comedies.—

> Our wooing doth not end like an old play ;
> Jack hath not Jill :

and Shakespeare strikes a passionate note across
it at last, in the entrance of the messenger, who
announces to the princess that the king her father
is suddenly dead.

The merely dramatic interest of the piece is
slight enough ; only just sufficient, indeed, to
form the vehicle of its wit and poetry.   The
scene—a park of the King of Navarre—is
unaltered throughout ; and the unity of the

[1] Act V. Scene II.

play is not so much the unity of a drama as
that of a series of pictorial groups, in which
the same figures reappear, in different combina-
tions but on the same background. It is as if
Shakespeare had intended to bind together, by
some inventive conceit, the devices of an ancient
tapestry, and give voices to its figures. On one
side, a fair palace ; on the other, the tents of
the Princess of France, who has come on an
embassy from her father to the King of Navarre ;
in the midst, a wide space of smooth grass.
The same personages are combined over and
over again into a series of gallant scenes—the
princess, the three masked ladies, the quaint,
pedantic king ; one of those amiable kings men
have never loved enough, whose serious occupa-
tion with the things of the mind seems, by
contrast with the more usual forms of kingship,
like frivolity or play. Some of the figures are
grotesque merely, and all the male ones at least,
a little fantastic. Certain objects reappearing
from scene to scene—love-letters crammed with
verses to the margin, and lovers' toys—hint
obscurely at some story of intrigue. Between
these groups, on a smaller scale, come the
slighter and more homely episodes, with Sir
Nathaniel the curate, the country-maid Jaque-
netta, Moth or Mote the elfin-page, with Hiems
and Ver, who recite "the dialogue that the
two learned men have compiled in praise
of the owl and the cuckoo." The ladies are

lodged in tents, because the king, like the princess
of the modern poet's fancy, has taken a vow

To make his court a little Academe,

and for three years' space no woman may come
within a mile of it ; and the play shows how
this artificial attempt was broken through. For
the king and his three fellow-scholars are of
course soon forsworn, and turn to writing sonnets,
each to his chosen lady. These fellow-scholars
of the king—"quaint votaries of science" at
first, afterwards "affection's men-at-arms"—three
youthful knights, gallant, amorous, chivalrous,
but also a little affected, sporting always a
curious foppery of language, are, throughout,
the leading figures in the foreground ; one of
them, in particular, being more carefully de-
picted than the others, and in himself very
noticeable—a portrait with somewhat puzzling
manner and expression, which at once catches
the eye irresistibly and keeps it fixed.

Play is often that about which people are
most serious ; and the humourist may observe
how, under all love of playthings, there is
almost always hidden an appreciation of something really engaging and delightful. This is
true always of the toys of children : it is often
true of the playthings of grown-up people,
their vanities, their fopperies even, their lighter
loves ; the cynic would add their pursuit of
fame. Certainly, this is true without exception

of the playthings of a past age, which to those
who succeed it are always full of a pensive
interest—old manners, old dresses, old houses.
For what is called fashion in these matters
occupies, in each age, much of the care of many
of the most discerning people, furnishing them
with a kind of mirror of their real inward refinements, and their capacity for selection. Such
modes or fashions are, at their best, an example
of the artistic predominance of form over matter ;
of the manner of the doing of it over the thing
done ; and have a beauty of their own. It is
so with that old euphuism of the Elizabethan
age—that pride of dainty language and curious
expression, which it is very easy to ridicule,
which often made itself ridiculous, but which
had below it a real sense of fitness and nicety ;
and which, as we see in this very play, and still
more clearly in the Sonnets, had some fascination
for the young Shakespeare himself. It is this
foppery of delicate language, this fashionable
plaything of his time, with which Shakespeare
is occupied in *Love's Labours Lost*. He shows
us the manner in all its stages ; passing from the
grotesque and vulgar pedantry of Holofernes,
through the extravagant but polished caricature
of Armado, to become the peculiar characteristic
of a real though still quaint poetry in Biron
himself, who is still chargeable even at his best
with just a little affectation. As Shakespeare
laughs broadly at it in Holofernes or Armado, so he

is the analyst of its curious charm in Biron ; and this analysis involves a delicate raillery by Shakespeare himself at his own chosen manner.

This "foppery" of Shakespeare's day had, then, its really delightful side, a quality in no sense "affected," by which it satisfies a real instinct in our minds—the fancy so many of us have for an exquisite and curious skill in the use of words. Biron is the perfect flower of this manner :

> A man of fire-new words, fashion's own knight :

—as he describes Armado, in terms which are really applicable to himself.   In him this manner blends with a true gallantry of nature, and an affectionate complaisance and grace.   He has at times some of its extravagance or caricature also, but the shades of expression by which he passes from this to the " golden cadence " of Shakespeare's own most characteristic verse, are so fine, that it is sometimes difficult to trace them.   What is a vulgarity in Holofernes, and a caricature in Armado, refines itself with him into the expression of a nature truly and inwardly bent upon a form of delicate perfection, and is accompanied by a real insight into the laws which determine what is exquisite in language, and their root in the nature of things.   He can appreciate quite the opposite style—

> In russet yeas, and honest kersey noes ;

he knows the first law of pathos, that

> Honest plain words best suit the ear of grief.

He delights in his own rapidity of intuition ;
and, in harmony with the half-sensuous philosophy of the Sonnets, exalts, a little scornfully,
in many memorable expressions, the judgment
of the senses, above all slower, more toilsome
means of knowledge, scorning some who fail to
see things only because they are so clear :

> So ere you find where light in darkness lies,
> Your light grows dark by losing of your eyes :—

as with some German commentators on Shakespeare. Appealing always to actual sensation
from men's affected theories, he might seem to
despise learning ; as, indeed, he has taken up
his deep studies partly in sport, and demands
always the profit of learning in renewed enjoyment. Yet he surprises us from time to time by
intuitions which could come only from a deep
experience and power of observation ; and men
listen to him, old and young, in spite of themselves. He is quickly impressible to the slightest
clouding of the spirits in social intercourse, and
has his moments of extreme seriousness : his
trial-task may well be, as Rosaline puts it—

> To enforce the pained impotent to smile.

But still, through all, he is true to his chosen
manner : that gloss of dainty language is a
second nature with him : even at his best he
is not without a certain artifice : the trick
of playing on words never deserts him ; and

APPRECIATIONS

Shakespeare, in whose own genius there is an element of this very quality, shows us in this graceful, and, as it seems, studied, portrait, his enjoyment of it.

As happens with every true dramatist, Shakespeare is for the most part hidden behind the persons of his creation. Yet there are certain of his characters in which we feel that there is something of self-portraiture. And it is not so much in his grander, more subtle and ingenious creations that we feel this—in *Hamlet* and *King Lear*—as in those slighter and more spontaneously developed figures, who, while far from playing principal parts, are yet distinguished by a peculiar happiness and delicate ease in the drawing of them ; figures which possess, above all, that winning attractiveness which there is no man but would willingly exercise, and which resemble those works of art which, though not meant to be very great or imposing, are yet wrought of the choicest material. Mercutio, in *Romeo and Juliet*, belongs to this group of Shakespeare's characters—versatile, mercurial people, such as make good actors, and in whom the

Nimble spirits of the arteries,

the finer but still merely animal elements of great wit, predominate. A careful delineation of minor, yet expressive traits seems to mark them out as the characters of his predilection ;

168

and it is hard not to identify him with these more than with others. Biron, in *Love's Labours Lost*, is perhaps the most striking member of this group. In this character, which is never quite in touch, never quite on a perfect level of understanding, with the other persons of the play, we see, perhaps, a reflex of Shakespeare himself, when he has just become able to stand aside from and estimate the first period of his poetry.

1878.

"MEASURE FOR MEASURE"

In *Measure for Measure*, as in some other of his plays, Shakespeare has remodelled an earlier and somewhat rough composition to "finer issues," suffering much to remain as it had come from the less skilful hand, and not raising the whole of his work to an equal degree of intensity. Hence perhaps some of that depth and weightiness which make this play so impressive, as with the true seal of experience, like a fragment of life itself, rough and disjointed indeed, but forced to yield in places its profounder meaning. In *Measure for Measure*, in contrast with the flawless execution of *Romeo and Juliet*, Shakespeare has spent his art in just enough modification of the scheme of the older play to make it exponent of this purpose, adapting its terrible essential incidents, so that Coleridge found it the only painful work among Shakespeare's dramas, and leaving for the reader of to-day more than the usual number of difficult expressions ; but infusing a lavish colour and a profound significance into it, so that under his

touch certain select portions of it rise far above
the level of all but his own best poetry, and
working out of it a morality so characteristic
that the play might well pass for the central
expression of his moral judgments. It remains
a comedy, as indeed is congruous with the bland,
half-humorous equity which informs the whole
composition, sinking from the heights of sorrow
and terror into the rough scheme of the earlier
piece ; yet it is hardly less full of what is really
tragic in man's existence than if Claudio had
indeed "stooped to death." Even the humorous concluding scenes have traits of special grace,
retaining in less emphatic passages a stray line
or word of power, as it seems, so that we watch
to the end for the traces where the nobler hand
has glanced along, leaving its vestiges, as if
accidentally or wastefully, in the rising of the
style.

The interest of *Measure for Measure*, therefore,
is partly that of an old story told over again.
We measure with curiosity that variety of
resources which has enabled Shakespeare to
refashion the original material with a higher
motive ; adding to the intricacy of the piece, yet
so modifying its structure as to give the whole
almost the unity of a single scene ; lending, by
the light of a philosophy which dwells much on
what is complex and subtle in our nature, a true
human propriety to its strange and unexpected
turns of feeling and character, to incidents so

difficult as the fall of Angelo, and the subsequent
reconciliation of Isabella, so that she pleads suc-
cessfully for his life. It was from Whetstone, a
contemporary English writer, that Shakespeare
derived the outline of Cinthio's "rare history"
of *Promos and Cassandra*, one of that numerous
class of Italian stories, like Boccaccio's *Tancred
of Salerno*, in which the mere energy of southern
passion has everything its own way, and which,
though they may repel many a northern reader
by a certain crudity in their colouring, seem to
have been full of fascination for the Elizabethan
age. This story, as it appears in Whetstone's
endless comedy, is almost as rough as the roughest
episode of actual criminal life. But the play
seems never to have been acted, and some time
after its publication Whetstone himself turned
the thing into a tale, included in his *Heptameron
of Civil Discourses*, where it still figures as a
genuine piece, with touches of undesigned poetry,
a quaint field-flower here and there of diction
or sentiment, the whole strung up to an effective
brevity, and with the fragrance of that admirable
age of literature all about it. Here, then, there
is something of the original Italian colour : in
this narrative Shakespeare may well have caught
the first glimpse of a composition with nobler
proportions ; and some artless sketch from his
own hand, perhaps, putting together his first impressions, insinuated itself between Whetstone's
work and the play as we actually read it. Out

of these insignificant sources Shakespeare's play rises, full of solemn expression, and with a profoundly designed beauty, the new body of a higher, though sometimes remote and difficult poetry, escaping from the imperfect relics of the old story, yet not wholly transformed, and even as it stands but the preparation only, we might think, of a still more imposing design. For once we have in it a real example of that sort of writing which is sometimes described as *suggestive*, and which by the help of certain subtly calculated hints only, brings into distinct shape the reader's own half-developed imaginings. Often the quality is attributed to writing merely vague and unrealised, but in *Measure for Measure*, quite certainly, Shakespeare has directed the attention of sympathetic readers along certain channels of meditation beyond the immediate scope of his work.

Measure for Measure, therefore, by the quality of these higher designs, woven by his strange magic on a texture of poorer quality, is hardly less indicative than *Hamlet* even, of Shakespeare's reason, of his power of moral interpretation. It deals, not like *Hamlet* with the problems which beset one of exceptional temperament, but with mere human nature. It brings before us a group of persons, attractive, full of desire, vessels of the genial, seed-bearing powers of nature, a gaudy existence flowering out over the old court and city of Vienna, a spectacle of the fulness and pride of life which to some may seem to touch the verge of wantonness. Behind this group of people, behind their various action, Shakespeare inspires in us the sense of a strong tyranny of nature and circumstance. Then what shall there be on this side of it—on our side, the spectators' side, of this painted screen, with its puppets who are really glad or sorry all the time ? what philosophy of life, what sort of equity ?

Stimulated to read more carefully by Shakespeare's own profounder touches, the reader will note the vivid reality, the subtle interchange of light and shade, the strongly contrasted characters of this group of persons, passing across the stage so quickly. The slightest of them is at least not ill-natured : the meanest of them can put forth a plea for existence— *Truly, sir, I am a poor fellow that would live !*— they are never sure of themselves, even in the strong tower of a cold unimpressible nature : they are capable of many friendships and of a true dignity in danger, giving each other a sympathetic, if transitory, regret—one sorry that another "should be foolishly lost at a game of tick-tack." Words which seem to exhaust man's deepest sentiment concerning death and life are put on the lips of a gilded, witless youth ; and the saintly Isabella feels fire creep along her, kindling her tongue to eloquence at the suggestion of shame. In places the shadow deepens : death intrudes itself on the scene, as among other things " a great disguiser," blanching the features of youth and spoiling its goodly hair, touching the fine Claudio even with its disgraceful associations. As in Orcagna's fresco at Pisa, it comes capriciously, giving many and long reprieves to Barnardine, who has been waiting for it nine years in prison, taking another thence by fever, another by mistake of judgment, embracing others in the midst of their music and song. The little mirror of existence, which reflects to each for a moment the stage on which he plays, is broken at last by a capricious accident ; while all alike, in their yearning for untasted enjoyment, are really discounting their days, grasping so hastily and accepting so inexactly the precious pieces. The Duke's quaint but excellent moralising at the beginning of the third act does but express, like the chorus of a Greek play, the spirit of the passing incidents. To him in Shakespeare's play, to a few here and there in the actual world, this strange practical paradox of our life, so unwise in its eager haste, reveals itself in all its clearness.

The Duke disguised as a friar, with his curious moralising on life and death, and Isabella in her first mood of renunciation, a thing " ensky'd and sainted," come with the quiet of the cloister as a relief to this lust and pride of life : like some grey monastic picture hung on the wall of a gaudy room, their presence cools the heated air of the piece. For a moment we

are within the placid conventual walls, whither
they fancy at first that the Duke has come as a
man crossed in love, with Friar Thomas and
Friar Peter, calling each other by their homely,
English names, or at the nunnery among the
novices, with their little limited privileges, where

> If you speak you must not show your face,
> Or if you show your face you must not speak.

Not less precious for this relief in the general
structure of the piece, than for its own peculiar
graces is the episode of Mariana, a creature
wholly of Shakespeare's invention, told, by way
of interlude, in subdued prose. The moated
grange, with its dejected mistress, its long, list-
less, discontented days, where we hear only the
voice of a boy broken off suddenly in the midst
of one of the loveliest songs of Shakespeare,
or of Shakespeare's school,[1] is the pleasantest of
many glimpses we get here of pleasant places—the
field without the town, Angelo's garden-house, the
consecrated fountain. Indirectly it has suggested
two of the most perfect compositions among the
poetry of our own generation. Again it is a
picture within a picture, but with fainter lines
and a greyer atmosphere : we have here the same
passions, the same wrongs, the same continuance
of affection, the same crying out upon death, as
in the nearer and larger piece, though softened,
and reduced to the mood of a more dreamy scene.

[1] Fletcher, in the *Bloody Brother*, gives the rest of it.

"MEASURE FOR MEASURE"

Of Angelo we may feel at first sight inclined to say only *guarda e passa !* or to ask whether he is indeed psychologically possible. In the old story, he figures as an embodiment of pure and unmodified evil, like " Hyliogabalus of Rome or Denis of Sicyll." But the embodiment of pure evil is no proper subject of art, and Shakespeare, in the spirit of a philosophy which dwells much on the complications of outward circumstance with men's inclinations, turns into a subtle study in casuistry this incident of the austere judge fallen suddenly into utmost corruption by a momentary contact with supreme purity. But the main interest in *Measure for Measure* is not, as in *Promos and Cassandra*, in the relation of Isabella and Angelo, but rather in the relation of Claudio and Isabella.

Greek tragedy in some of its noblest products has taken for its theme the love of a sister, a sentiment unimpassioned indeed, purifying by the very spectacle of its passionlessness, but capable of a fierce and almost animal strength if informed for a moment by pity and regret. At first Isabella comes upon the scene as a tranquillising influence in it. But Shakespeare, in the development of the action, brings quite different and unexpected qualities out of her. It is his characteristic poetry to expose this cold, chastened personality, respected even by the worldly Lucio as "something ensky'd and sainted, and almost an immortal spirit," to two sharp, shameful trials, and wring out of her a fiery, revealing eloquence. Thrown into the terrible dilemma of the piece, called upon to sacrifice that cloistral whiteness to sisterly affection, become in a moment the ground of strong, contending passions, she develops a new character and shows herself suddenly of kindred with those strangely conceived women, like Webster's Vittoria, who unite to a seductive sweetness something of a dangerous and tigerlike changefulness of feeling. The swift, vindictive anger leaps, like a white flame, into this white spirit, and, stripped in a moment of all convention, she stands before us clear, detached, columnar, among the tender frailties of the piece. Cassandra, the original of Isabella in Whetstone's tale, with the purpose of the Roman Lucretia in her mind, yields gracefully enough to the conditions of her brother's safety; and to the lighter reader of Shakespeare there may seem something harshly conceived, or psychologically impossible even, in the suddenness of the change wrought in her, as Claudio welcomes for a moment the chance of life through her compliance with Angelo's will, and he may have a sense here of flagging skill, as in words less finely handled than in the preceding scene. The play, though still not without traces of nobler handiwork, sinks down, as we know, at last into almost homely comedy, and it might be supposed that just here the grander manner

deserted it. But the skill with which Isabella
plays upon Claudio's well-recognised sense of
honour, and endeavours by means of that to
insure him beforehand from the acceptance of
life on baser terms, indicates no coming laxity
of hand just in this place. It was rather that
there rose in Shakespeare's conception, as there
may for the reader, as there certainly would in
any good acting of the part, something of that
terror, the seeking for which is one of the notes
of romanticism in Shakespeare and his circle.
The stream of ardent natural affection, poured
as sudden hatred upon the youth condemned to
die, adds an additional note of expression to the
horror of the prison where so much of the
scene takes place. It is not here only that
Shakespeare has conceived of such extreme
anger and pity as putting a sort of genius into
simple women, so that their "lips drop eloquence," and their intuitions interpret that
which is often too hard or fine for manlier
reason; and it is Isabella with her grand imaginative diction, and that poetry laid upon the
"prone and speechless dialect" there is in mere
youth itself, who gives utterance to the equity,
the finer judgments of the piece on men and
things.

From behind this group with its subtle
lights and shades, its poetry, its impressive
contrasts, Shakespeare, as I said, conveys to us
a strong sense of the tyranny of nature and

circumstance over human action. The most powerful expressions of this side of experience might be found here. The bloodless, impassible temperament does but wait for its opportunity, for the almost accidental coherence of time with place, and place with wishing, to annul its long and patient discipline, and become in a moment the very opposite of that which under ordinary conditions it seemed to be, even to itself. The mere resolute self-assertion of the blood brings to others special temptations, temptations which, as defects or over-growths, lie in the very qualities which make them otherwise imposing or attractive; the very advantage of men's gifts of intellect or sentiment being dependent on a balance in their use so delicate that men hardly maintain it always. Something also must be conceded to influences merely physical, to the complexion of the heavens, the skyey influences, shifting as the stars shift; as something also to the mere caprice of men exercised over each other in the dispensations of social or political order, to the chance which makes the life or death of Claudio dependent on Angelo's will.

The many veins of thought which render the poetry of this play so weighty and impressive unite in the image of Claudio, a flowerlike young man, whom, prompted by a few hints from Shakespeare, the imagination easily clothes with all the bravery of youth, as he crosses the stage before us on his way to death, coming so hastily to the end of his pilgrimage. Set in the horrible blackness of the prison, with its various forms of unsightly death, this flower seems the braver. Fallen by " prompture of the blood," the victim of a suddenly revived law against the common fault of youth like his, he finds his life forfeited as if by the chance of a lottery. With that instinctive clinging to life, which breaks through the subtlest casuistries of monk or sage apologising for an early death, he welcomes for a moment the chance of life through his sister's shame, though he revolts hardly less from the notion of perpetual imprisonment so repulsive to the buoyant energy of youth. Familiarised, by the words alike of friends and the indifferent, to the thought of death, he becomes gentle and subdued indeed, yet more perhaps through pride than real resignation, and would go down to darkness at last hard and unblinded. Called upon suddenly to encounter his fate, looking with keen and resolute profile straight before him, he gives utterance to some of the central truths of human feeling, the sincere, concentrated expression of the recoiling flesh. Thoughts as profound and poetical as Hamlet's arise in him ; and but for the accidental arrest of sentence he would descend into the dust, a mere gilded, idle flower of youth indeed, but with what are perhaps the most eloquent of all Shakespeare's words upon his lips.

As Shakespeare in *Measure for Measure* has

refashioned, after a nobler pattern, materials already at hand, so that the relics of other men's poetry are incorporated into his perfect work, so traces of the old "morality," that early form of dramatic composition which had for its function the inculcating of some moral theme, survive in it also, and give it a peculiar ethical interest. This ethical interest, though it can escape no attentive reader, yet, in accordance with that artistic law which demands the predominance of form everywhere over the mere matter or subject handled, is not to be wholly separated from the special circumstances, necessities, embarrassments, of these particular dramatic persons. The old "moralities" exemplified most often some rough-and-ready lesson. Here the very intricacy and subtlety of the moral world itself, the difficulty of seizing the true relations of so complex a material, the difficulty of just judgment, of judgment that shall not be unjust, are the lessons conveyed. Even in Whetstone's old story this peculiar vein of moralising comes to the surface : even there, we notice the tendency to dwell on mixed motives, the contending issues of action, the presence of virtues and vices alike in unexpected places, on "the hard choice of two evils," on the "imprisoning" of men's "real intents." *Measure for Measure* is full of expressions drawn from a profound experience of these casuistries, and that ethical interest becomes predominant in it : it is no longer *Promos and*

"MEASURE FOR MEASURE"

Cassandra, but *Measure for Measure*, its new name expressly suggesting the subject of *poetical justice*. The action of the play, like the action of life itself for the keener observer, develops in us the conception of this poetical justice, and the yearning to realise it, the true justice of which Angelo knows nothing, because it lies for the most part beyond the limits of any acknowledged law. The idea of justice involves the idea of rights. But at bottom rights are equivalent to that which really is, to facts ; and the recognition of his rights therefore, the justice he requires of our hands, or our thoughts, is the recognition of that which the person, in his inmost nature, really is ; and as sympathy alone can discover that which really is in matters of feeling and thought, true justice is in its essence a finer knowledge through love.

> 'Tis very pregnant :
> The jewel that we find we stoop and take it,
> Because we see it ; but what we do not see
> We tread upon, and never think of it.

It is for this finer justice, a justice based on a more delicate appreciation of the true conditions of men and things, a true respect of persons in our estimate of actions, that the people in *Measure for Measure* cry out as they pass before us ; and as the poetry of this play is full of the peculiarities of Shakespeare's poetry, so in its ethics it is an epitome of Shakespeare's moral judgments. They are the moral judgments of

an observer, of one who sits as a spectator, and
knows how the threads in the design before him
hold together under the surface : they are the
judgments of the humourist also, who follows
with a half-amused but always pitiful sympathy,
the various ways of human disposition, and sees
less distance than ordinary men between what
are called respectively great and little things.
It is not always that poetry can be the exponent
of morality ; but it is this aspect of morals which
it represents most naturally, for this true justice
is dependent on just those finer appreciations
which poetry cultivates in us the power of
making, those peculiar valuations of action and
its effect which poetry actually requires.

1874.

SHAKESPEARE'S ENGLISH KINGS

A brittle glory shineth in this face :
As brittle as the glory is the face.

THE English plays of Shakespeare needed but
the completion of one unimportant interval to
possess the unity of a popular chronicle from
Richard the Second to Henry the Eighth, and
possess, as they actually stand, the unity of a
common motive in the handling of the various
events and persons which they bring before us.
Certain of his historic dramas, not English, display Shakespeare's mastery in the development
of the heroic nature amid heroic circumstances ;
and had he chosen, from English history, to deal
with Cœur-de-Lion or Edward the First, the
innate quality of his subject would doubtless
have called into play something of that profound
and sombre power which in *Julius Cæsar* and
Macbeth has sounded the depths of mighty
character. True, on the whole, to fact, it is
another side of kingship which he has made
prominent in his English histories. The irony

of kingship—average human nature, flung with
a wonderfully pathetic effect into the vortex
of great events ; tragedy of everyday quality
heightened in degree only by the conspicuous
scene which does but make those who play
their parts there conspicuously unfortunate ; the
utterance of common humanity straight from the
heart, but refined like other common things for
kingly uses by Shakespeare's unfailing eloquence:
such, unconsciously for the most part, though
palpably enough to the careful reader, is the conception under which Shakespeare has arranged
the lights and shadows of the story of the
English kings, emphasising merely the light
and shadow inherent in it, and keeping very
close to the original authorities, not simply in
the general outline of these dramatic histories
but sometimes in their very expression. Certainly the history itself, as he found it in
Hall, Holinshed, and Stowe, those somewhat
picturesque old chroniclers who had themselves
an eye for the dramatic " effects " of human life,
has much of this sentiment already about it.
What he did not find there was the natural
prerogative—such justification, in kingly, that is
to say, in exceptional, qualities, of the exceptional
position, as makes it practicable in the result.
It is no *Henriade* he writes, and no history of
the English people, but the sad fortunes of some
English kings as conspicuous examples of the
ordinary human condition. As in a children's

story, all princes are in extremes. Delightful in the sunshine above the wall into which chance lifts the flower for a season, they can but plead somewhat more touchingly than others their everyday weakness in the storm. Such is the motive that gives unity to these unequal and intermittent contributions toward a slowly evolved dramatic chronicle, which it would have taken many days to rehearse ; a not distant story from real life still well remembered in its general course, to which people might listen now and again, as long as they cared, finding human nature at least wherever their attention struck ground in it.

He begins with John, and allows indeed to the first of these English kings a kind of greatness, making the development of the play centre in the counteraction of his natural gifts—that something of heroic force about him—by a madness which takes the shape of reckless impiety, forced especially on men's attention by the terrible circumstances of his end, in the delineation of which Shakespeare triumphs, setting, with true poetic tact, this incident of the king's death, in all the horror of a violent one, amid a scene delicately suggestive of what is perennially peaceful and genial in the outward world. Like the sensual humours of Falstaff in another play, the presence of the bastard Faulconbridge, with his physical energy and his unmistakable family likeness—"those limbs

a

which Sir Robert never holp to make " [1]—
contributes to an almost coarse assertion of the
force of nature, of the somewhat ironic pre-
ponderance of nature and circumstance over
men's artificial arrangements, to the recognition
of a certain potent natural aristocracy, which is
far from being always identical with that more
formal, heraldic one. And what is a coarse fact
in the case of Faulconbridge becomes a motive
of pathetic appeal in the wan and babyish Arthur.
The magic with which nature models tiny and
delicate children to the likeness of their rough
fathers is nowhere more justly expressed than in
the words of King Philip.—

> Look here upon thy brother Geoffrey's face !
> These eyes, these brows were moulded out of his :
> This little abstract doth contain that large
> Which died in Geoffrey ; and the hand of time
> Shall draw this brief into as huge a volume.

It was perhaps something of a boyish memory
of the shocking end of his father that had
distorted the piety of Henry the Third into
superstitious terror. A frightened soul, himself
touched with the contrary sort of religious
madness, doting on all that was alien from his
father's huge ferocity, on the genialities, the soft
gilding, of life, on the genuine interests of art
and poetry, to be credited more than any other
person with the deep religious expression of

Elinor. Do you not read some tokens of my son (Cœur-de-Lion)
In the large composition of this man ?

SHAKESPEARE'S ENGLISH KINGS

Westminster Abbey, Henry the Third, picturesque though useless, but certainly touching,
might have furnished Shakespeare, had he filled
up this interval in his series, with precisely the
kind of effect he tends towards in his English
plays. But he found it completer still in the
person and story of Richard the Second, a figure
—"that sweet lovely rose"—which haunts
Shakespeare's mind, as it seems long to have
haunted the minds of the English people, as the
most touching of all examples of the irony of
kingship.

Henry the Fourth—to look for a moment
beyond our immediate subject, in pursuit of
Shakespeare's thought—is presented, of course,
in general outline, as an impersonation of "surviving force : " he has a certain amount of
kingcraft also, a real fitness for great opportunity.
But still true to his leading motive, Shakespeare,
in *King Henry the Fourth*, has left the high-water
mark of his poetry in the soliloquy which represents royalty longing vainly for the toiler's
sleep ; while the popularity, the showy heroism,
of Henry the Fifth, is used to give emphatic
point to the old earthy commonplace about
"wild oats." The wealth of homely humour
in these plays, the fun coming straight home to
all the world, of Fluellen especially in his unconscious interview with the king, the boisterous
earthiness of Falstaff and his companions, con-
tribute to the same effect. The keynote of

APPRECIATIONS

Shakespeare's treatment is indeed expressed by Henry the Fifth himself, the *greatest* of Shakespeare's kings.—"Though I speak it to you," he says *incognito*, under cover of night, to a common soldier on the field, " I think the king is but a man, as I am : the violet smells to him as it doth to me : all his senses have but human conditions ; and though his affections be higher mounted than ours yet when they stoop they stoop with like wing." And, in truth, the really kingly speeches which Shakespeare assigns to him, as to other kings weak enough in all but speech, are but a kind of flowers, worn for, and effective only as personal embellishment. They combine to one result with the merely outward and ceremonial ornaments of royalty, its pageantries, flaunting so naively, so credulously, in Shakespeare, as in that old medieval time. And then, the force of Hotspur is but transient youth, the common heat of youth, in him. The character of Henry the Sixth again, *roi fainéant*, with La Pucelle[1] for his counterfoil, lay in the direct course of Shakespeare's design : he has done much to fix the sentiment of the " holy Henry." Richard the Third, touched, like John, with an effect of real heroism, is spoiled like him by something of criminal madness, and reaches his highest level of tragic expression

---

[1] Perhaps the one person of *genius* in these English plays.
> The spirit of deep prophecy she hath,
> Exceeding the nine Sibyls of old Rome :
> What's past and what's to come she can descry.

when circumstances reduce him to terms of
mere human nature.—

> A horse ! A horse ! My kingdom for a horse !

The Princes in the Tower recall to mind the lot of
young Arthur :—

> I'll go with thee,
> And find the inheritance of this poor child,
> His little kingdom of a forced grave.

And when Shakespeare comes to Henry the
Eighth, it is not the superficial though very
English splendour of the king himself, but
the really potent and ascendant nature of the
butcher's son on the one hand, and Katharine's
subdued reproduction of the sad fortunes of
Richard the Second on the other, that define
his central interest.[1]

With a prescience of the Wars of the Roses,
of which his errors were the original cause, it
is Richard who best exposes Shakespeare's own
constant sentiment concerning war, and especially
that sort of civil war which was then recent in
English memories. The soul of Shakespeare,
certainly, was not wanting in a sense of the
magnanimity of warriors. The grandiose aspects
of war, its magnificent apparelling, he records

---

[1] Proposing in this paper to trace the leading sentiment in
Shakespeare's English Plays as a sort of *popular dramatic chronicle*,
I have left untouched the question how much (or, in the case of
Henry the Sixth and *Henry the Eighth*, how little) of them may be
really his : how far inferior hands have contributed to a result, true
on the whole to the greater, that is to say, the Shakespearian
elements in them.

monumentally enough—the "dressing of the lists," the lion's heart, its unfaltering haste thither in all the freshness of youth and morning.—

> Not sick although I have to do with death—
> The sun doth gild our armour : Up, my Lords!—
> I saw young Harry with his beaver on,
> His cuisses on his thighs, gallantly arm'd,
> Rise from the ground like feather'd Mercury.

Only, with Shakespeare, the afterthought is immediate :—

> They come like sacrifices in their trim.

—Will it never be to-day ? I will trot to-morrow a mile, and my way shall be paved with English faces.

This sentiment Richard reiterates very plaintively, in association with the delicate sweetness of the English fields, still sweet and fresh, like London and her other fair towns in that England of Chaucer, for whose soil the exiled Bolingbroke is made to long so dangerously, while Richard on his return from Ireland salutes it—

> That pale, that white-fac'd shore,—
> As a long-parted mother with her child.—
> So, weeping, smiling, greet I thee, my earth !
> And do thee favour with my royal hands.—

Then (of Bolingbroke)

> Ere the crown he looks for live in peace,
> Ten thousand bloody crowns of mothers' sons
> Shall ill become the flower of England's face ;
> Change the complexion of her maid-pale peace
> To scarlet indignation, and bedew
> My pastures' grass with faithful English blood.—

SHAKESPEARE'S ENGLISH KINGS

Why have they dared to march ?—

asks York,

So many miles upon her peaceful bosom,
Frighting her pale-fac'd visages with war ?—

waking, according to Richard,

Our peace, which in our country's cradle,
Draws the sweet infant breath of gentle sleep :—

bedrenching " with crimson tempest "

The fresh green lap of fair king Richard's land :—

frighting "fair peace" from "our quiet confines,"
laying

The summer's dust with showers of blood,
Rained from the wounds of slaughter'd Englishmen :

bruising

Her flowerets with the armed hoofs
Of hostile paces.

Perhaps it is not too fanciful to note in this
play a peculiar recoil from the mere instruments
of warfare, the contact of the " rude ribs," the
" flint bosom," of Barkloughly Castle or Pomfret
or

Julius Cæsar's ill-erected tower :

the

Boisterous untun'd drums
With harsh-resounding trumpets' dreadful bray
And grating shock of wrathful iron arms.

It is as if the lax, soft beauty of the king took
effect, at least by contrast, on everything beside.
One gracious prerogative, certainly, Shake-

speare's English kings possess : they are a very
eloquent company, and Richard is the most
sweet-tongued of them all. In no other play
perhaps is there such a flush of those gay, fresh,
variegated flowers of speech—colour and figure,
not lightly attached to, but fused into, the very
phrase itself—which Shakespeare cannot help
dispensing to his characters, as in this " play of
the Deposing of King Richard the Second," an
exquisite poet if he is nothing else, from first to
last, in light and gloom alike, able to see all
things poetically, to give a poetic turn to his
conduct of them, and refreshing with his golden
language the tritest aspects of that ironic contrast
between the pretensions of a king and the actual
necessities of his destiny. What a garden of
words ! With him, blank verse, infinitely graceful, deliberate, musical in inflexion, becomes
indeed a true " verse royal," that rhyming lapse,
which to the Shakespearian ear, at least in youth,
came as the last touch of refinement on it, being
here doubly appropriate. His eloquence blends
with that fatal beauty, of which he was so frankly
aware, so amiable to his friends, to his wife, of
the effects of which on the people his enemies
were so much afraid, on which Shakespeare himself dwells so attentively as the " royal blood "
comes and goes in the face with his rapid
changes of temper. As happens with sensitive
natures, it attunes him to a congruous suavity of
manners, by which anger itself became flattering:

194

it blends with his merely youthful hopefulness and high spirits, his sympathetic love for gay people, things, apparel—" his cote of gold and stone, valued at thirty thousand marks," the novel Italian fashions he preferred, as also with those real amiabilities that made people forget the darker touches of his character, but never tire of the pathetic rehearsal of his fall, the meekness of which would have seemed merely abject in a less graceful performer.

Yet it is only fair to say that in the painstaking " revival" of *King Richard the Second*, by the late Charles Kean, those who were very young thirty years ago were afforded much more than Shakespeare's play could ever have been before—the very person of the king based on the stately old portrait in Westminster Abbey, " the earliest extant contemporary likeness of any English sovereign," the grace, the winning pathos, the sympathetic voice of the player, the tasteful archæology confronting vulgar modern London with a scenic reproduction, for once really agreeable, of the London of Chaucer. In the hands of Kean the play became like an exquisite performance on the violin.

The long agony of one so gaily painted by nature's self, from his " tragic abdication " till the hour in which he

> Sluiced out his innocent soul thro' streams of blood,

was for playwrights a subject ready to hand, and
195

became early the theme of a popular drama,
of which some have fancied surviving favourite
fragments in the rhymed parts of Shakespeare's
work.

> The king Richard of Yngland
> Was in his flowris then regnand :
> But his flowris efter sone
> Fadyt, and ware all undone :—

says the old chronicle. Strangely enough,
Shakespeare supposes him an over-confident
believer in that divine right of kings, of which
people in Shakespeare's time were coming to
hear so much ; a general right, sealed to him
(so Richard is made to think) as an ineradicable
personal gift by the touch—stream rather, over
head and breast and shoulders—of the "holy
oil" of his consecration at Westminster ; not,
however, through some oversight, the genuine
balm used at the coronation of his successor,
given, according to legend, by the Blessed Virgin
to Saint Thomas of Canterbury. Richard himself found that, it was said, among other forgotten treasures, at the crisis of his changing
fortunes, and vainly sought reconsecration therewith—understood, wistfully, that it was reserved
for his happier rival. And yet his coronation,
by the pageantry, the amplitude, the learned
care, of its order, so lengthy that the king, then
only eleven years of age, and fasting, as a com-
municant at the ceremony, was carried away in
a faint, fixed the type under which it has ever

since continued. And nowhere is there so emphatic a reiteration as in *Richard the Second* of
the sentiment which those singular rites were
calculated to produce.

> Not all the water in the rough rude sea
> Can wash the balm from an anointed king,—

as supplementing another, almost supernatural,
right.—"Edward's seven sons," of whom
Richard's father was one,

> Were as seven phials of his sacred blood.

But this, too, in the hands of Shakespeare,
becomes for him, like any other of those
fantastic, ineffectual, easily discredited, personal
graces, as capricious in its operation on men's
wills as merely physical beauty, kindling himself
to eloquence indeed, but only giving double
pathos to insults which "barbarism itself"
might have pitied—the dust in his face, as he
returns, through the streets of London, a prisoner
in the train of his victorious enemy.

> How soon my sorrow hath destroyed my face!

he cries, in that most poetic invention of the
mirror scene, which does but reinforce again
that physical charm which all confessed. The
sense of "divine right" in kings is found to act
not so much as a secret of power over others, as
of infatuation to themselves. And of all those
personal gifts the one which alone never altogether fails him is just that royal utterance, his

appreciation of the poetry of his own hapless lot,
an eloquent self-pity, infecting others in spite
of themselves, till they too become irresistibly
eloquent about him.

In the Roman Pontifical, of which the order
of Coronation is really a part, there is no form
for the inverse process, no rite of "degradation," such as that by which an offending priest
or bishop may be deprived, if not of the essential
quality of "orders," yet, one by one, of its outward dignities. It is as if Shakespeare had had
in mind some such inverted rite, like those old
ecclesiastical or military ones, by which human
hardness, or human justice, adds the last touch
of unkindness to the execution of its sentences,
in the scene where Richard "deposes" himself,
as in some long, agonising ceremony, reflectively
drawn out, with an extraordinary refinement of
intelligence and variety of piteous appeal, but
also with a felicity of poetic invention, which
puts these pages into a very select class, with the
finest "vermeil and ivory" work of Chatterton or
Keats.

> Fetch hither Richard that in common view
> He may surrender !—

And Richard more than concurs : he throws himself into the part, realises a type, falls gracefully
as on the world's stage.—Why is he sent for ?

> To do that office of thine own good will
> Which tired majesty did make thee offer.—

> Now mark me ! how I will undo myself.

SHAKESPEARE'S ENGLISH KINGS

" Hath Bolingbroke deposed thine intellect ? "
the Queen asks him, on his way to the Tower :—

> Hath Bolingbroke
> Deposed thine intellect? hath he been in thy heart?

And in truth, but for that adventitious poetic gold,
it would be only " plume-plucked Richard."

> I find myself a traitor with the rest,
> For I have given here my soul's consent
> To undeck the pompous body of a king.

He is duly reminded, indeed, how

> That which in mean men we entitle patience
> Is pale cold cowardice in noble breasts.

Yet at least within the poetic bounds of Shakespeare's play, through Shakespeare's bountiful gifts,
his desire seems fulfilled.—

> O ! that I were as great
> As is my grief.

And his grief becomes nothing less than a
central expression of all that in the revolutions
of Fortune's wheel goes *down* in the world.

No ! Shakespeare's kings are not, nor are
meant to be, great men : rather, little or quite
ordinary humanity, thrust upon greatness, with
those pathetic results, the natural self-pity of
the weak heightened in them into irresistible
appeal to others as the net result of their royal
prerogative. One after another, they seem to
lie composed in Shakespeare's embalming pages,
with just that touch of nature about them,

making the whole world akin, which has infused into their tombs at Westminster a rare poetic grace. It is that irony of kingship, the sense that it is in its happiness child's play, in its sorrows, after all, but children's grief, which gives its finer accent to all the changeful feeling of these wonderful speeches :—the great meekness of the graceful, wild creature, tamed at last.—

> Give Richard leave to live till Richard die !

his somewhat abject fear of death, turning to acquiescence at moments of extreme weariness :—

> My large kingdom for a little grave !
> A little little grave, an obscure grave !—

his religious appeal in the last reserve, with its bold reference to the judgment of Pilate, as he thinks once more of his " anointing."

And as happens with children he attains contentment finally in the merely passive recognition of superior strength, in the naturalness of the result of the great battle as a matter of course, and experiences something of the royal prerogative of poetry to obscure, or at least to attune and soften men's griefs. As in some sweet anthem of Handel, the sufferer, who put finger to the organ under the utmost pressure of mental conflict, extracts a kind of peace at last from the mere skill with which he sets his distress to music.—

> Beshrew thee, Cousin, that didst lead me forth
> Of that sweet way I was in to despair !

SHAKESPEARE'S ENGLISH KINGS

" With Cain go wander through the shades
of night ! "—cries the new king to the gaoler
Exton, dissimulating his share in the murder
he is thought to have suggested ; and in truth
there is something of the murdered Abel about
Shakespeare's Richard.   The fact seems to be
that he died of " waste and a broken heart : " it
was by way of proof that his end had been a
natural one that, stifling a real fear of the face,
the face of Richard, on men's minds, with the
added pleading now of all dead faces, Henry
exposed the corpse to general view ; and
Shakespeare, in bringing it on the stage, in the
last scene of his play, does but follow out the
motive with which he has emphasised Richard's
physical beauty all through it—that "most
beauteous inn," as the Queen says quaintly,
meeting him on the way to death—residence,
then soon to be deserted, of that wayward,
frenzied, but withal so affectionate soul.
Though the body did not go to Westminster
immediately, his tomb,

That small model of the barren earth
Which serves as paste and cover to our bones,[1]

the effigy clasping the hand of his youthful
consort, was already prepared there, with " rich

[1] Perhaps a *double entendre :*—of any ordinary grave, as com-
prising, in effect, the whole small earth now left to its occupant :
or, of such a tomb as Richard's in particular, with its actual model,
or effigy, of the clay of him. Both senses are so characteristic
that it would be a pity to lose either.

gilding and ornaments," monument of poetic regret, for Queen Anne of Bohemia, not of course
the " Queen " of Shakespeare, who however seems
to have transferred to this second wife something of Richard's wildly proclaimed affection
for the first.   In this way, through the connecting link of that sacred spot, our thoughts once
more associate Richard's two fallacious preroga-
tives, his personal beauty and his " anointing."

According to Johnson, *Richard the Second* is
one of those plays which Shakespeare has
" apparently revised ; " and how doubtly delightful Shakespeare is where he seems to have
revised !   " Would that he had blotted a
thousand "—a thousand hasty phrases, we may
venture once more to say with his earlier critic,
now that the tiresome German superstition has
passed away which challenged us to a dogmatic
faith in the plenary verbal inspiration of every
one of Shakespeare's clowns.   Like some melo-
diously contending anthem of Handel's, I said,
of Richard's meek " undoing " of himself in
the mirror-scene ; and, in fact, the play of
Richard the Second does, like a musical composition, possess a certain concentration of all its parts,
a simple continuity, an evenness in execution,
which are rare in the great dramatist.   With
Romeo and Juliet, that perfect symphony (symphony of three independent poetic forms set in
a grander one [1] which it is the merit of German

[1] The Sonnet : the Aubade : the Epithalamium.

criticism to have detected) it belongs to a small
group of plays, where, by happy birth and consistent evolution, dramatic form approaches to
something like the unity of a lyrical ballad, a
lyric, a song, a single strain of music.   Which
sort of poetry we are to account the highest,
is perhaps a barren question. Yet if, in art
generally, unity of impression is a note of what
is perfect, then lyric poetry, which in spite of
complex structure often preserves the unity of a
single passionate ejaculation, would rank higher
than dramatic poetry, where, especially to the
reader, as distinguished from the spectator
assisting at a theatrical performance, there must
always be a sense of the effort necessary to keep
the various parts from flying asunder, a sense of
imperfect continuity, such as the older criticism
vainly sought to obviate by the rule of the
dramatic " unities."   It follows that a play
attains artistic perfection just in proportion as it
approaches that unity of lyrical effect, as if a
song or ballad were still lying at the root of it,
all the various expression of the conflict of
character and circumstance falling at last into the
compass of a single melody, or musical theme.
As, historically, the earliest classic drama arose
out of the chorus, from which this or that person,
this or that episode, detached itself, so, into the
unity of a choric song the perfect drama ever
tends to return, its intellectual scope deepened,
complicated, enlarged, but still with an unmistak-

able singleness, or identity, in its impression on the mind. Just there, in that vivid single impression left on the mind when all is over, not in any mechanical limitation of time and place, is the secret of the " unities "—the true imaginative unity—of the drama.

1889.

DANTE GABRIEL ROSSETTI

It was characteristic of a poet who had ever something about him of mystic isolation, and will still appeal perhaps, though with a name it may seem now established in English literature, to a special and limited audience, that some of his poems had won a kind of exquisite fame before they were in the full sense published. *The Blessed Damozel*, although actually printed twice before the year 1870, was eagerly circulated in manuscript ; and the volume which it now opens came at last to satisfy a long-standing curiosity as to the poet, whose pictures also had become an object of the same peculiar kind of interest. For those poems were the work of a painter, understood to belong to, and to be indeed the leader, of a new school then rising into note ; and the reader of to-day may observe already, in *The Blessed Damozel*, written at the age of eighteen, a prefigurement of the chief characteristics of that school, as he will recognise in it also, in proportion as he really knows Rossetti, many of the characteristics which are most markedly personal and his own. Common

to that school and to him, and in both alike of
primary significance, was the quality of sincerity,
already felt as one of the charms of that earliest
poem—a perfect sincerity, taking effect in the
deliberate use of the most direct and unconven-
tional expression, for the conveyance of a poetic
sense which recognised no conventional standard
of what poetry was called upon to be. At a
time when poetic originality in England might
seem to have had its utmost play, here was certainly one new poet more, with a structure and
music of verse, a vocabulary, an accent, unmistakably novel, yet felt to be no mere tricks of manner
adopted with a view to forcing attention—an
accent which might rather count as the very
seal of reality on one man's own proper speech ;
as that speech itself was the wholly natural
expression of certain wonderful things he really
felt and saw. Here was one, who had a matter
to present to his readers, to himself at least, in
the first instance, so valuable, so real and definite,
that his primary aim, as regards form or expression in his verse, would be but its exact equival-
ence to those *data* within. That he had this
gift of transparency in language—the control of
a style which did but obediently shift and shape
itself to the mental motion, as a well-trained
hand can follow on the tracing-paper the outline of an original drawing below it, was proved
afterwards by a volume of typically perfect
translations from the delightful but difficult

DANTE GABRIEL ROSSETTI

" early Italian poets " : such transparency being indeed the secret of all genuine style, of all such style as can truly belong to one man and not to another. His own meaning was always personal and even recondite, in a certain sense learned and casuistical, sometimes complex or obscure ; but the term was always, one could see, deliberately chosen from many competitors, as the just transcript of that peculiar phase of soul which he alone knew, precisely as he knew it.

One of the peculiarities of *The Blessed Damozel* was a definiteness of sensible imagery, which seemed almost grotesque to some, and was strange, above all, in a theme so profoundly visionary. The gold bar of heaven from which she leaned, her hair yellow like ripe corn, are but examples of a general treatment, as naively detailed as the pictures of those early painters contemporary with Dante, who has shown a similar care for minute and definite imagery in his verse ; there, too, in the very midst of profoundly mystic vision. Such definition of outline is indeed one among many points in which Rossetti resembles the great Italian poet, of whom, led to him at first by family circumstances, he was ever a lover—a " servant and singer," faithful as Dante, " of Florence and of Beatrice "—with some close inward conformities of genius also, independent of any mere circumstances of education. It was said by a critic of the last century, not wisely though agreeably to the practice of his time, that poetry rejoices in abstractions. For Rossetti, as for Dante, without question on his part, the first condition of the poetic way of seeing and presenting things is particularisation. "Tell me now," he writes, for Villon's

> Dictes-moy où, n'en quel pays,
> Est Flora, la belle Romaine—
>
> Tell me now, in what hidden way is
> Lady Flora the lovely Roman :

—"way," in which one might actually chance to meet her ; the unmistakably poetic effect of the couplet in English being dependent on the definiteness of that single word (though actually lighted on in the search after a difficult double rhyme) for which every one else would have written, like Villon himself, a more general one, just equivalent to place or region.

And this delight in concrete definition is allied with another of his conformities to Dante, the really imaginative vividness, namely, of his personifications—his hold upon them, or rather their hold upon him, with the force of a Frankenstein, when once they have taken life from him. Not Death only and Sleep, for instance, and the winged spirit of Love, but certain particular aspects of them, a whole "populace" of special hours and places, "the hour" even "which might have been, yet might not be," are living creatures, with hands and eyes and articulate voices.

DANTE GABRIEL ROSSETTI

Stands it not by the door—
Love's Hour—till she and I shall meet;
With bodiless form and unapparent feet
That cast no shadow yet before,
Though round its head the dawn begins to pour
The breath that makes day sweet?—

Nay, why
Name the dead hours? I mind them well:
Their ghosts in many darkened doorways dwell
With desolate eyes to know them by.

Poetry as a *mania*—one of Plato's two higher forms of "divine" mania—has, in all its species, a mere insanity incidental to it, the "defect of its quality," into which it may lapse in its moment of weakness; and the insanity which follows a vivid poetic anthropomorphism like that of Rossetti may be noted here and there in his work, in a forced and almost grotesque materialising of abstractions, as Dante also became at times a mere subject of the scholastic realism of the Middle Age.

In *Love's Nocturn* and *The Stream's Secret*, congruously perhaps with a certain feverishness of soul in the moods they present, there is at times a near approach (may it be said?) to such insanity of realism—

Pity and love shall burn
In her pressed cheek and cherishing hands;
And from the living spirit of love that stands
Between her lips to soothe and yearn,
Each separate breath shall clasp me round in turn
And loose my spirit's bands.

But even if we concede this ; even if we allow,
in the very plan of those two compositions,
something of the literary conceit—what exquisite, what novel flowers of poetry, we must
admit them to be, as they stand ! In the one,
what a delight in all the natural beauty of water,
all its details for the eye of a painter ; in the
other, how subtle and fine the imaginative hold
upon all the secret ways of sleep and dreams !
In both of them, with much the same attitude
and tone, Love—sick and doubtful Love—would
fain inquire of what lies below the surface of
sleep, and below the water ; stream or dream
being forced to speak by Love's powerful " control " ; and the poet would have it foretell the
fortune, issue, and event of his wasting passion.
Such artifices, indeed, were not unknown in the
old Provençal poetry of which Dante had learned
something. Only, in Rossetti at least, they are
redeemed by a serious purpose, by that sincerity
of his, which allies itself readily to a serious
beauty, a sort of grandeur of literary workman-
ship, to a great style. One seems to hear there
a really new kind of poetic utterance, with effects
which have nothing else like them ; as there is
nothing else, for instance, like the narrative of
Jacob's Dream in *Genesis*, or Blake's design of
the Singing of the Morning Stars, or Addison's
Nineteenth Psalm.

With him indeed, as in some revival of
the old mythopœic age, common things—dawn,

noon, night—are full of human or personal expression, full of sentiment. The lovely little sceneries scattered up and down his poems, glimpses of a landscape, not indeed of broad open-air effects, but rather that of a painter concentrated upon the picturesque effect of one or two selected objects at a time—the " hollow brimmed with mist," or the " ruined weir," as he sees it from one of the windows, or reflected in one of the mirrors of his " house of life " (the vignettes for instance seen by Rose Mary in the magic beryl) attest, by their very freshness and simplicity, to a pictorial or descriptive power in dealing with the inanimate world, which is certainly also one half of the charm, in that other, more remote and mystic, use of it. For with Rossetti this sense of lifeless nature, after all, is translated to a higher service, in which it does but incorporate itself with some phase of strong emotion. Every one understands how this may happen at critical moments of life ; what a weirdly expressive soul may have crept, even in full noonday, into " the white-flower'd elder-thicket," when Godiva saw it " gleam through the Gothic archways in the wall," at the end of her terrible ride. To Rossetti it is so always, because to him life is a crisis at every moment. A sustained impressibility towards the mysterious conditions of man's everyday life, towards the very mystery itself in it, gives a singular gravity to all his work : those matters never became trite

to him.   But throughout, it is the ideal intensity
of love—of love based upon a perfect yet peculiar
type of physical or material beauty—which is
enthroned in the midst of those mysterious
powers ; Youth and Death, Destiny and Fortune,
Fame, Poetic Fame, Memory, Oblivion, and the
like.   Rossetti is one of those who, in the words
of Mérimée, *se passionnent pour la passion*, one of
Love's lovers.

And yet, again as with Dante, to speak of his
ideal type of beauty as material, is partly misleading.   Spirit and matter, indeed, have been
for the most part opposed, with a false contrast
or antagonism by schoolmen, whose artificial
creation those abstractions really are.   In our
actual concrete experience, the two trains of
phenomena which the words *matter* and *spirit*
do but roughly distinguish, play inextricably into
each other.   Practically, the church of the
Middle Age by its æsthetic worship, its sacra-
mentalism, its real faith in the resurrection of
the flesh, had set itself against that Manichean
opposition of spirit and matter, and its results in
men's way of taking life ; and in this, Dante is
the central representative of its spirit.   To
him, in the vehement and impassioned heat
of his conceptions, the material and the
spiritual are fused and blent : if the spiritual
attains the definite visibility of a crystal, what
is material loses its earthiness and impurity.
And here again, by force of instinct, Rossetti

DANTE GABRIEL ROSSETTI

is one with him.   His chosen type of beauty is
one,

> Whose speech Truth knows not from her thought,
> Nor Love her body from her soul.

Like Dante, he knows no region of spirit which
shall not be sensuous also, or material. The
shadowy world, which he realises so powerfully,
has still the ways and houses, the land and water,
the light and darkness, the fire and flowers, that
had so much to do in the moulding of those
bodily powers and aspects which counted for so
large a part of the soul, here.

For Rossetti, then, the great affections of
persons to each other, swayed and determined,
in the case of his highly pictorial genius, mainly
by that so-called material loveliness, formed the
great undeniable reality in things, the solid
resisting substance, in a world where all beside
might be but shadow. The fortunes of those
affections—of the great love so determined ; its
casuistries, its languor sometimes ; above all, its
sorrows ; its fortunate or unfortunate collisions
with those other great matters ; how it looks, as
the long day of life goes round, in the light and
shadow of them : all this, conceived with an
abundant imagination, and a deep, a philosophic,
reflectiveness, is the matter of his verse, and
especially of what he designed as his chief poetic
work, " a work to be called *The House of Life*,"
towards which the majority of his sonnets and
songs were contributions.

APPRECIATIONS

The dwelling-place in which one finds oneself by chance or destiny, yet can partly fashion for oneself ; never properly one's own at all, if it be changed too lightly ; in which every object has its associations—the dim mirrors, the portraits, the lamps, the books, the hair-tresses of the dead and visionary magic crystals in the secret drawers, the names and words scratched on the windows, windows open upon prospects the saddest or the sweetest ; the house one must quit, yet taking perhaps, how much of its quietly active light and colour along with us !—grown now to be a kind of raiment to one's body, as the body, according to Swedenborg, is but the raiment of the soul — under that image, the whole of Rossetti's work might count as a *House of Life*, of which he is but the " Interpreter." And it is a " haunted " house. A sense of power in love, defying distance, and those barriers which are so much more than physical distance, of unutterable desire penetrating into the world of sleep, however " lead-bound," was one of those anticipative notes obscurely struck in *The Blessed Damozel*, and, in his later work, makes him speak sometimes almost like a believer in mesmerism. Dream-land, as we said, with its " phantoms of the body," deftly coming and going on love's service, is to him, in no mere fancy or figure of speech, a real country, a veritable expansion of, or addition to, our waking life ; and he did well perhaps to wait carefully upon sleep, for the lack of it became mortal disease with him. One may even recognise a sort of morbid and over-hasty making-ready for death itself, which increases on him ; thoughts concerning it, its imageries, coming with a frequency and importunity, in excess, one might think, of even the very saddest, quite wholesome wisdom.

And indeed the publication of his second volume of *Ballads and Sonnets* preceded his death by scarcely a twelvemonth. That volume bears witness to the reverse of any failure of power, or falling-off from his early standard of literary perfection, in every one of his then accustomed forms of poetry—the song, the sonnet, and the ballad. The newly printed sonnets, now completing *The House of Life*, certainly advanced beyond those earlier ones, in clearness ; his dramatic power in the ballad, was here at its height ; while one monumental, gnomic piece, *Soothsay*, testifies, more clearly even than the *Nineveh* of his first volume, to the reflective force, the dry reason, always at work behind his imaginative creations, which at no time dispensed with a genuine intellectual structure. For in matters of pure reflection also, Rossetti maintained the painter's sensuous clearness of conception ; and this has something to do with the capacity, largely illustrated by his ballads, of telling some red-hearted story of impassioned action with effect.

Have there, in very deed, been ages, in which

the external conditions of poetry such as Rossetti's were of more spontaneous growth than in our own ? The archaic side of Rossetti's work, his preferences in regard to earlier poetry, connect him with those who have certainly thought so, who fancied they could have breathed more largely in the age of Chaucer, or of Ronsard, in one of those ages, in the words of Stendhal— *ces siècles de passions où les âmes pouvaient se livrer franchement à la plus haute exaltation, quand les passions qui font la possibilité comme les sujets des beaux arts existaient.* We may think, perhaps, that such old time as that has never really existed except in the fancy of poets ; but it was to find it, that Rossetti turned so often from modern life to the chronicle of the past. Old Scotch history, perhaps beyond any other, is strong in the matter of heroic and vehement hatreds and love, the tragic Mary herself being but the perfect blossom of them ; and it is from that history that Rossetti has taken the subjects of the two longer ballads of his second volume : of the three admirable ballads in it, *The King's Tragedy* (in which Rossetti has dexterously inter-woven some relics of James's own exquisite early verse) reaching the highest level of dramatic success, and marking perfection, perhaps, in this kind of poetry ; which, in the earlier volume, gave us, among other pieces, *Troy Town, Sister Helen,* and *Eden Bower.*

Like those earlier pieces, the ballads of the

second volume bring with them the question of the poetic value of the " refrain "—

> Eden bower's in flower :
> And O the bower and the hour !

—and the like. Two of those ballads—*Troy Town* and *Eden Bower*, are terrible in theme ; and the refrain serves, perhaps, to relieve their bold aim at the sentiment of terror. In *Sister Helen* again, the refrain has a real, and sustained purpose (being here duly varicd also) and performs the part of a chorus, as the story proceeds. Yet even in these cases, whatever its effect may be in actual recitation, it may fairly be questioned, whether, to the mere reader their actual effect is not that of a positive interruption and drawback, at least in pieces so lengthy ; and Rossetti himself, it would seem, came to think so, for in the shortest of his later ballads, *The White Ship*—that old true history of the generosity with which a youth, worthless in life, flung himself upon death —he was contented with a single utterance of the refrain, " given out" like the keynote or tune of a chant.

In *The King's Tragedy*, Rossetti has worked upon motive, broadly human (to adopt the phrase of popular criticism) such as one and all may realise. Rossetti, indeed, with all his self-concentration upon his own peculiar aim, by no means ignored those general interests which are external to poetry as he conceived it ; as he has

shown here and there, in this poetic, as also in
pictorial, work. It was but that, in a life to be
shorter even than the average, he found enough
to occupy him in the fulfilment of a task, plainly
" given him to do." Perhaps, if one had to
name a single composition of his to readers
desiring to make acquaintance with him for the
first time, one would select: *The King's Tragedy*
—that poem so moving, so popularly dramatic,
and lifelike. Notwithstanding this, his work,
it must be conceded, certainly through no
narrowness or egotism, but in the faithfulness of
a true workman to a vocation so emphatic, was
mainly of the esoteric order. But poetry, at all
times, exercises two distinct functions : it may
reveal, it may unveil to every eye, the ideal
aspects of common things, after Gray's way
(though Gray too, it is well to remember, seemed
in his own day, seemed even to Johnson, obscure)
or it may actually add to the number of motives
poetic and uncommon in themselves, by the
imaginative creation of things that are ideal from
their very birth. Rossetti did something, something excellent, of the former kind ; but his
characteristic, his really revealing work, lay in
the adding to poetry of fresh poetic material, of
a new order of phenomena, in the creation of a
new ideal.

1883.

FEUILLET'S "LA MORTE"

In his latest novel M. Octave Feuillet adds two charming people to that chosen group of personages in which he loves to trace the development of the more serious elements of character amid the refinements and artifices of modern society, and which make such good company. The proper function of fictitious literature in affording us a refuge into a world slightly better—better conceived, or better finished—than the real one, is effected in most instances less through the imaginary events at which a novelist causes us to assist, than by the imaginary persons to whom he introduces us. The situations of M. Feuillet's novels are indeed of a real and intrinsic importance :—tragic crises, inherent in the general conditions of human nature itself, or which arise necessarily out of the special conditions of modern society. Still, with him, in the actual result, they become subordinate, as it is their tendency to do in real life, to the characters they help to form. Often, his most attentive reader will have forgotten the actual details of his plot; while

the soul, tried, enlarged, shaped by it, remains as
a well-fixed type in the memory. He may return
a second or third time to *Sibylle*, or *Le Journal d'une
Femme*, or *Les Amours de Philippe*, and watch, surprised afresh, the clean, dainty, word-sparing
literary operation (word-sparing, yet with no loss
of real grace or ease) which, sometimes in a few
pages, with the perfect logic of a problem of
Euclid, complicates and then unravels some
moral embarrassment, really worthy of a trained
dramatic expert. But the characters themselves,
the agents in those difficult, revealing situations,
such a reader will recognise as old acquaintances
after the first reading, feeling for them as for some
gifted and attractive persons he has known in the
actual world—Raoul de Chalys, Henri de Lerne,
Madame de Técle, Jeanne de la Roche-Ermel,
Maurice de Frémeuse, many others ; to whom
must now be added Bernard and Aliette de
Vaudricourt.

" How I love those people ! " cries Mademoiselle de Courteheuse, of Madame de Sévigné
and some other of her literary favourites in the
days of the Grand Monarch. " What good
company ! What pleasure they took in high
things ! How much more worthy they were
than the people who live now ! "—What good
company ! That is precisely what the admirer
of M. Feuillet's books feels as one by one he
places them on his book-shelf, to be sought again.
What is proposed here is not to tell his last story,

but to give the English reader specimens of his most recent effort at characterisation.

It is with the journal of Bernard himself that the story opens, September 187-. Bernard-Maurice Hugon de Montauret, Vicomte de Vaudricourt, is on a visit to his uncle, the head of his family, at La Savinière, a country-house somewhere between Normandy and Brittany. This uncle, an artificial old Parisian in manner, but honest in purpose, a good talker, and full of real affection for his heir Bernard, is one of M. Feuillet's good minor characters—one of the quietly humorous figures with which he relieves his more serious company. Bernard, with whom the refinements of a man of fashion in the Parisian world by no means disguise a powerful intelligence cultivated by wide reading, has had thoughts during his tedious stay at La Savinière of writing a history of the reign of Louis the Fourteenth, the library of a neighbouring *château* being rich in memoirs of that period. Finally, he prefers to write his own story, a story so much more interesting to himself; to write it at a peculiar crisis in his life, the moment when his uncle, unmarried, but anxious to perpetuate his race, is bent on providing him with a wife, and indeed has one in view.

The accomplished Bernard, with many graces of person, by his own confession, takes nothing seriously. As to that matter of religious beliefs, " the breeze of the age, and of science, has blown over him, as it has blown over his contemporaries, and left empty space there." Still, when he saw his childish religious faith departing from him, as he thinks it must necessarily depart from all intelligent male Parisians, he wept. Since that moment, however, a gaiety, serene and imperturbable, has been the mainstay of his happily constituted character. The girl to whom his uncle desires to see him united—odd, quixotic, intelligent, with a sort of pathetic and delicate grace, and herself very religious—belongs to an old-fashioned, devout family, resident at Varaville, near by. M. Feuillet, with half a dozen fine touches of his admirable pencil makes us see the place. And the enterprise has at least sufficient interest to keep Bernard in the country, which the young Parisian detests. "This piquant episode of my life," he writes, "seems to me to be really deserving of study; to be worth etching off, day by day, by an observer well informed on the subject."

Recognising in himself, though as his one real fault, that he can take nothing seriously in heaven or earth, Bernard de Vaudricourt, like all M. Feuillet's favourite young men, so often erring or corrupt, is a man of scrupulous "honour." He has already shown disinterestedness in wishing his rich uncle to marry again. His friends at Varaville think so well-mannered a young man more of a Christian than he really is; and, at all events, he will never owe his happiness to a falsehood. If he has great faults, hypocrisy at least is no part of them. In oblique paths he finds himself ill at ease. Decidedly, as he thinks, he was born for straight ways, for loyalty in all his enterprises ; and he congratulates himself upon the fact.

In truth, Bernard has merits which he ignores, at least in this first part of his journal: merits which are necessary to explain the influence he is able to exercise from the first over such a character as Mademoiselle de Courteheuse. His charm, in fact, is in the union of that gay and apparently wanton nature with a genuine power of appreciating devotion in others, which becomes devotion in himself. With all the much-cherished elegance and worldly glitter of his personality, he is capable of apprehending, of understanding and being touched by the presence of great matters. In spite of that happy lightness of heart, so jealously fenced about, he is to be wholly caught at last, as he is worthy to be, by the serious, the generous influence of things. In proportion to his immense worldly strength is his capacity for the immense pity which breaks his heart.

In a few life-like touches M. Feuillet brings out, as if it were indeed a thing of ordinary existence, the simple yet delicate life of a French country-house, the ideal life in an ideal France. Bernard is paying a morning visit at the old turreted home of the "prehistoric" Courteheuse family. Mademoiselle Aliette de Courteheuse, a studious girl, though a bold and excellent rider

APPRECIATIONS

—Mademoiselle de Courteheuse, " with her hair of that strange colour of fine ashes "—has conducted her visitor to see the library :

One day she took me to see the library, rich in works of the seventeenth century and in memoirs relating to that time. I remarked there also a curious collection of engravings of the same period. "Your father," I observed, "had a strong predilection for the age of Louis the Fourteenth."

" My father lived in that age," she answered gravely. And as I looked at her with surprise, and a little embarrassed, she added, " He made me live there too, in his company."

And then the eyes of this singular girl filled with tears. She turned away, took a few steps to suppress her emotion, and returning, pointed me to a chair. Then seating herself on the step of the book-case, she said, " I must explain my father to you."

She was half a minute collecting her thoughts : then, speaking with an expansion of manner not habitual with her, hesitating, and blushing deeply, whenever she was about to utter a word that might seem a shade too serious for lips so youthful :—" My father," she proceeded, " died of the consequences of a wound he had received at Patay. That may show you that he loved his country, but he was no lover of his own age. He possessed in the highest degree the love of order ; and order was a thing nowhere to be seen. He had a horror of disorder ; and he saw it everywhere. In those last years, especially, his reverence, his beliefs, his tastes, all alike were ruffled to the point of actual suffering, by whatever was done and said and written around him. Deeply saddened by the conditions of the present time, he habituated himself to find a refuge in the past, and the seventeenth century more particularly offered him the kind of society in which he would have wished to live—a society, well-ordered, polished, lettered, believing. More and more he loved to shut himself up in it. More and more also he loved to make the moral discipline and the literary tastes of that favourite age prevail in his own household. You may even have remarked that he carried his predilection into minute matters of arrangement and decoration. You can see from this window the straight paths, the box in patterns, the yew trees and clipped alleys of our garden. You may notice that in our garden-beds we have none but flowers of the period—lilies, rose-mallows, immortelles, rose-pinks, in short what people call parsonage flowers—*des fleurs de curé.* Our old silvan tapestries, similarly, are of that age. You see too that all our furniture, from presses and sideboards, down to our little tables and our arm-chairs, is in the severest style of Louis the Fourteenth. My father did not appreciate the dainty research of our modern luxury. He maintained that our excessive care for the comforts of life weakened mind as well as body. That," added the girl with a laugh, —"that is why you find your chair so hard when you come to see us."

Then, with resumed gravity—" It was thus that my father endeavoured, by the very aspect and arrangement of outward things, to promote in himself the imaginary presence of the epoch in which his thoughts delighted. As for myself—need I tell you that I was the confidant of that father, so well-beloved : a confidant touched by his sorrows, full of indignation at his disappointments, charmed by his consolations. Here, precisely—surrounded by those books which we read together, and which he taught me to love—it is here that I have passed the pleasantest hours of my youth. In common we indulged our enthusiasm for those days of faith ; of the quiet life ; its blissful hours of leisure well-secured; for the French language in its beauty and purity ; the delicate, the noble urbanity, which was then the honour and the special mark of our country, but has ceased to be so."

She paused, with a little confusion, as I thought, at the warmth of her last words.

And then, just to break the silence, " You have explained," I said, "an impression which I have experienced again and again in my visits here, and which has sometimes reached the intensity of an actual illusion, though a very agreeable one. The look of your house, its style, its tone and keeping, carried me two centuries back so completely that I should hardly have been surprised to hear Monsieur le Prince, Madame de la Fayette, or Madame de Sévigné herself, announced at your drawing-room door."

"Would it might be ! " said Mademoiselle de Courteheuse.

APPRECIATIONS

"Ah! Monsieur, how I love those people! What good company! What pleasure they took in high things! How much more worthy they were than the people who live now!" I tried to calm a little this retrospective enthusiasm, so much to the prejudice of my contemporaries and of myself. "Most truly, Mademoiselle," I said, "the age which you regret had its rare merits—merits which I appreciate as you do. But then, need one say that that society, so regular, so choice in appearance, had, like our own, below the surface, its troubles, its disorders? I see here many of the memoirs of that time. I can't tell exactly which of them you may or may not have read, and so I feel a certain difficulty in speaking."

She interrupted me: "Ah!" she said, with entire simplicity, "I understand you. I have not read all you see here. But I have read enough of it to know that my friends in that past age had, like those who live now, their passions, their weaknesses, their mistakes. But, as my father used to say to me, all that did but pass over a ground of what was solid and serious, which always discovered itself again anew. There were great faults then; but there were also great repentances. There was a certain higher region ·to which everything conducted— even what was evil." She blushed deeply: then rising a little suddenly, "A long speech!" she said: "Forgive me! I am not usually so very talkative. It is because my father was in question; and I should wish his memory to be as dear and as venerable to all the rest of the world as it is to me."

We pass over the many little dramatic intrigues and misunderstandings, with the more or less adroit interferences of the uncle, which raise and lower alternately Bernard's hopes. M. Feuillet has more than once tried his hand with striking success in the portraiture of French ecclesiastics. He has drawn none better than the Bishop of Saint-Méen, uncle of Mademoiselle de Courte-heuse, to whose interests he is devoted. Bernard feels that to gain the influence of this prelate would be to gain his cause ; and the opportunity for an interview comes.

Monseigneur de Courteheuse would seem to be little over fifty years of age : he is rather tall, and very thin : the eyes, black and full of life, are encircled by a ring of deep brown. His speech and gesture are animated, and, at times, as if carried away. He adopts frequently a sort of furious manner which on a sudden melts into the smile of an honest man. He has beautiful silvery hair, flying in vagrant locks over his forehead, and beautiful bishop's hands. As he becomes calm he has an imposing way of gently resettling himself in his sacerdotal dignity. To sum up : his is a physiognomy full of passion, consumed with zeal, yet still frank and sincere.

I was hardly seated, when with a motion of the hand he invited me to speak.

"Monseigneur !" I said, "I come to you (you understand me ?) as to my last resource. What I am now doing is almost an act of despair ; for it might seem at first sight that no member of the family of Mademoiselle de Courteheuse must show himself more pitiless than yourself towards the faults with which I am reproached. I am an unbeliever: you are an apostle ! And yet, Monseigneur, it is often at the hands of saintly priests, such as yourself, that the guilty find most indulgence. And then, I am not indeed guilty : I have but wandered. I am refused the hand of your niece because I do not share her faith — your own faith. But, Monseigneur, unbelief is not a crime, it is a misfortune. I know people often say, a man denies God when by his own conduct he has brought himself into a condition in which he may well desire that God does not exist. In this way he is made guilty, or, in a sense, responsible for his incredulity. For myself, Monseigneur, I have consulted my conscience with an entire sincerity ; and although my youth has been amiss, I am certain that my atheism proceeds from no sentiment of personal interest. On the contrary, I may tell you with truth that the day on which I perceived my faith come to nought, the day on which I lost hope in God, I shed the bitterest tears of my life. In spite of appearances, I am not so light a spirit as people think. I am not one of those for whom God, when He disappears, leaves no sense of a void place. Believe me!—a man may love sport, his club, his worldly habits, and yet have his hours of thought, of self-recollection. Do you suppose that in those hours one does not feel the frightful discomfort of an existence with no moral basis, without principles, with no outlook beyond this world? And yet, what can one do? You would tell me forthwith, in the goodness, the compassion, which I read in your eyes; Confide to me your objections to religion, and I will try to solve them. Monseigneur, I should hardly know how to answer you. My objections are 'Legion!' They are without number, like the stars in the sky: they come to us on all sides, from every quarter of the horizon, as if on the wings of the wind; and they leave in us, as they pass, ruins only, and darkness. Such has been my experience, and that of many others; and it has been as involuntary as it is irreparable."

"And I—Monsieur!" said the bishop, suddenly, casting on me one of his august looks, "Do you suppose that I am but a play-actor in my cathedral church?"

"Monseigneur!"

"Yes! Listening to you, one would suppose that we were come to a period of the world in which one must needs be either an atheist or a hypocrite! Personally, I claim to be neither one nor the other."

"Need I defend myself on that point, Monseigneur? Need I say that I did not come here to give you offence?"

"Doubtless! doubtless! Well, Monsieur, I admit;—not without great reserves, mind! for one is always more or less responsible for the atmosphere in which he lives, the influences to which he is subject, for the habitual turn he gives to his thoughts; still, I admit that you are the victim of the incredulity of the age, that you are altogether guiltless in your scepticism, your atheism! since you have no fear of hard words. Is it therefore any the less certain that the union of a fervent believer, such as my niece, with a man like yourself would be a moral disorder of which the consequences might be disastrous? Do you think it could be my duty, as a relative of Mademoiselle de Courteheuse, her spiritual father, as a prelate of the Church, to lend my hands to such disorder, to preside over the shocking union of two souls separated by the whole width of heaven?"

The bishop, in proposing that question, kept his eyes fixed ardently on mine.

"Monseigneur," I answered, after a moment's embarrassment, "you know as well as, and better than I, the condition of the world, and of our country, at this time. You know that unhappily I am not an exception : that men of faith are rare in it. And permit me to tell you my whole mind. If I must needs suffer the inconsolable misfortune of renouncing the happiness I had hoped for, are you quite sure that the man to whom one of these days you will give your niece may not be something more than a sceptic, or even an atheist ? "

"What, Monsieur ? "

" A hypocrite, Monseigneur ! Mademoiselle de Courteheuse is beautiful enough, rich enough, to excite the ambition of those who may be less scrupulous than I. As for me, if you now know that I am a sceptic, you know also that I am a man of honour : and there is something in that ! "

" A man of honour ! " the bishop muttered to himself, with a little petulance and hesitation. " A man of honour ! Yes, I believe it ! " Then, after an interval, " Come, Monsieur," he said gently, " your case is not as desperate as you suppose. My Aliette is one of those young enthusiasts through whom Heaven sometimes works miracles." And Bernard refusing any encouragement of that hope (the " very roots of faith are dead " in him for ever) " since you think that," the bishop answers, " it is honest to say so. But God has His ways ! "

Soon after, the journal comes to an end with that peculiar crisis in Bernard's life which had suggested the writing of it. Aliette, with the approval of her family, has given him her hand. Bernard accepts it with the full purpose of doing all he can to make his wife as happy as she is charming and beloved. The virginal first period of their married life in their dainty house in Paris — the pure and beautiful picture of the mother, the father, and at last the child, a little, girl, Jeanne—is presented with M. Feuillet's usual grace. Certain embarrassments succeed ; the development of what was ill-matched in their union ; but still with mutual loyalty. A far-reaching acquaintance with, and reflection upon, the world and its ways, especially the Parisian world, has gone into the apparently slight texture of these pages. The accomplished playwright may be recognised in the skilful touches with which M. Feuillet, unrivalled, as his regular readers know, in his power of breathing higher notes into the frivolous prattle of fashionable French life, develops the tragic germ in the elegant, youthful household. Amid the distractions of a society, frivolous, perhaps vulgar, Aliette's mind is still set on greater things ; and, in spite of a thousand rude discouragements, she maintains her generous hope for Bernard's restoration to faith. One day, a little roughly, he bids her relinquish that dream finally. She looks at him with the moist, suppliant eyes of some weak animal at bay. Then his native goodness returns. In a softened tone he owns himself wrong.

"As to conversions ;—no one must be despaired of. Do you remember M. de Rancé ? He lived in your favourite age ;—M. de Rancé. Well ! before he became the reformer of La Trappe he had been a worldling like me, and a great sceptic—what people called a libertine. Still he became a saint ! It is true he had a terrible reason for it. Do you know what it was converted him ? "

Aliette gave a sign that she did not know.

"Well ! he returned to Paris after a few days' absence. He

ran straight to the lady he loved ; Madame Montbazon, I think :
he went up a little staircase of which he had the key, and the
first thing he saw on the table in the middle of the room was
the head of his mistress, of which the doctors were about to
make a *post-mortem* examination."

"If I were sure," said Aliette, "that my head could have such
power, I would love to die."

She said it in a low voice, but with such an accent of loving
sincerity that her husband had a sensation of a sort of painful
disquiet. He smiled, however, and tapping her cheek softly,
"Folly !" he said. "A head, charming as yours, has no need
to be dead that it may work miracles !"

Certainly M. Feuillet has some weighty
charges to bring against the Parisian society of
our day. When Aliette revolts from a world of
gossip, which reduces all minds alike to the same
level of vulgar mediocrity, Bernard, on his side,
can perceive there a deterioration of moral tone
which shocks his sense of honour. As a man of
honour, he can hardly trust his wife to the
gaieties of a society which welcomes all the
world "to amuse itself in undress."

It happened that at this perplexed period in the youthful
household, one and the same person became the recipient both
of the tearful confidences of Madame de Vaudricourt and those
of her husband. It was the Duchess of Castel-Moret [she is
another of M. Feuillet's admirable minor sketches] an old
friend of the Vaudricourt family, and the only woman with
whom Aliette since her arrival in Paris had formed a kind of
intimacy. The Duchess was far from sharing, on points of
morality, and above all of religion, the severe and impassioned
orthodoxy of her young friend. She had lived, it is true, an
irreproachable life, but less in consequence of defined principles
than by instinct and natural taste. She admitted to herself
that she was an honest woman as a result of her birth, and had
no further merit in the matter. She was old, very careful of

herself, and a pleasant aroma floated about her, below her silvery hair. People loved her for her grace—the grace of another time than ours—for her wit, and her worldly wisdom, which she placed freely at the disposal of the public. Now and then she made a match : but her special gift lay rather in the way in which she came to the rescue when a marriage turned out ill. And she had no sinecure : the result was that she passed the best part of her time in repairing family rents. That might "last its time," she would say. "And then we know that what has been well mended sometimes lasts better than what is new."

A little later, Bernard, in the interest of Aliette, has chivalrously determined to quit Paris. At Valmoutiers, a fine old place in the neighbourhood of Fontainebleau, they established themselves for a country life. Here Aliette tastes the happiest days since her marriage. Bernard, of course, after a little time is greatly bored. But so far they have never seriously doubted of their great love for each other. It is here that M. Feuillet brings on the scene a kind of character new in his books ; perhaps hardly worthy of the other company there ; a sort of female Monsieur de Camors, but without his grace and tenderness, and who actually commits a crime. How would the morbid charms of M. de Camors have vanished, if, as his wife once suspected of him, he had ever contemplated crime ! And surely, the showy insolent charms of Sabine de Tallevaut, beautiful, intellectually gifted, supremely Amazonian, yet withal not drawn with M. Feuillet's usual fineness, scarcely hold out for the reader, any more than for

Bernard himself, in the long run, against the
vulgarising touch of her cold wickedness. Living
in the neighbourhood of Valmoutiers, in a somewhat melancholy abode (the mystery of which
in the eyes of Bernard adds to her poetic charm)
with her guardian, an old, rich, free-thinking doctor, devoted to research, she comes to
Valmoutiers one night in his company on the
occasion of the alarming illness of the only child.
They arrive escorted by Bernard himself. The
little Jeanne, wrapped in her coverlet, was placed
upon the table of her play-room, which was
illuminated as if for a party. The illness, the
operation (skilfully performed by the old doctor)
which restores her to life, are described with
that seemingly simple pathos in which M.
Feuillet's consummate art hides itself. Sabine
remains to watch the child's recovery, and
becomes an intimate. In vain Bernard struggles
against the first real passion of his life ;—does
everything but send its object out of his sight.
Aliette has divined their secret. In the fatal
illness which follows soon after, Bernard watches
over her with tender solicitude ; hoping against
hope that the disease may take a favourable turn.

"My child," he said to her one day, taking the hand which
she abandoned to him, " I have just been scolding old Victoire.
She is losing her head. In spite of the repeated assurances of
the doctors, she is alarmed at seeing you a little worse than
usual to-day, and has had the *Curé* sent for. Do you wish to
see him ? "

" Pray let me see him ! "

APPRECIATIONS

She sighed heavily, and fixed upon her husband her large blue eyes, full of anguish—an anguish so sharp and so singular that he felt frozen to the marrow.

He could not help saying with deep emotion, " Do you love me no longer, Aliette ? "

" For ever ! " murmured the poor child.

He leaned over her with a long kiss upon the forehead. She saw tears stealing from the eyes of her husband, and seemed as if surprised.

Soon afterwards Aliette is dead, to the profound sorrow of Bernard. Less than two years later he has become the husband of Mademoiselle Tallevaut. It was about two years after his marriage with Sabine that Bernard resumed the journal with which we began. In the pages which he now adds he seems at first unchanged. How then as to that story of M. de Rancé, the reformer of La Trappe, finding the head of his dead mistress ; an incident which the reader of *La Morte* will surely have taken as a " presentiment " ? Aliette had so taken it. " A head so charming as yours," Bernard had assured her tenderly, " does not need to be dead that it may work miracles ! "—How, in the few pages that remain, will M. Feuillet justify that, and certain other delicate touches of presentiment, and at the same time justify the title of his book ?

The journal is recommenced in February. On the twentieth of April Bernard writes, at Valmoutiers :

Under pretext of certain urgently needed repairs I am come to pass a week at Valmoutiers, and get a little pure air. By my orders they have kept Aliette's room under lock and key since the day when she left it in her coffin. To-day I re-entered it for the first time. There was a vague odour of her favourite perfumes. My poor Aliette! why was I unable, as you so ardently desired, to share your gentle creed, and associate myself to the life of your dreams, the life of honesty and peace? Compared with that which is mine to-day, it seems to me like paradise. What a terrible scene it was, here in this room! What a memory! I can still see the last look she fixed on me, a look almost of terror! and how quickly she died! I have taken the room for my own. But I shall not remain here long. I intend to go for a few days to Varaville. I want to see my little girl: her dear angel's face.

VALMOUTIERS, *April* 22.—What a change there has been in the world since my childhood: since my youth even! what a surprising change in so short a period, in the moral atmosphere we are breathing! Then we were, as it were, impregnated with the thought of God—a just God, but benevolent and fatherlike. We really lived under His eyes, as under the eyes of a parent, with respect and fear, but with confidence. We felt sustained by His invisible but undoubted presence. We spoke to Him, and it seemed that He answered. And now we feel ourselves alone—as it were abandoned in the immensity of the universe. We live in a world, hard, savage, full of hatred ; whose one cruel law is the struggle for existence, and in which we are no more than those natural elements, let loose to war with each other in fierce selfishness, without pity, with no appeal beyond, no hope of final justice. And above us, in place of the good God of our happy youth, nothing, any more! or worse than nothing—a deity, barbarous and ironical, who cares nothing at all about us.

The aged mother of Aliette, hitherto the guardian of his daughter, is lately dead. Bernard proposes to take the child away with him to Paris. The child's old nurse objects. On April the twenty-seventh, Bernard writes :

For a moment—for a few moments—in that room where I have been shutting myself up with the shadow of my poor

APPRECIATIONS

dead one, a horrible thought had come to me. I had driven it away as an insane fancy. But now,—yes! it is becoming a reality. Shall I write this? Yes! I will write it. It is my duty to do so; for from this moment the journal, begun in so much gaiety of heart, is but my last will and testament. If I should disappear from the world, the secret must not die with me. It must be bequeathed to the natural protectors of my child. Her interests, if not her life, are concerned therein.

Here, then, is what passed: I had not arrived in time to render my last duty to Madame de Courteheuse. The family was already dispersed. I found here only Aliette's brother. To him I communicated my plan concerning the child, and he could but approve. My intention was to bring away with Jeanne her nurse Victoire, who had brought her up, as she brought up her mother. But she is old, and in feeble health, and I feared some difficulties on her part; the more as her attitude towards myself since the death of my first wife has been marked by an ill grace approaching to hostility. I took her aside while Jeanne was playing in the garden.

"My good Victoire," I said, "while Madame de Courteheuse was living, I considered it a duty to leave her granddaughter in her keeping. Besides, no one was better fitted to watch over her education. At present my duty is to watch over it myself. I propose therefore to take Jeanne with me to Paris; and I hope that you may be willing to accompany her, and remain in her service." When she understood my intention, the old woman, in whose hands I had noticed a faint trembling, became suddenly very pale. She fixed her firm, grey eyes upon me: "Monsieur le Comte will not do that!"

"Pardon me, my good Victoire, that I shall do. I appreciate your good qualities of fidelity and devotion. I shall be very grateful if you will continue to take care of my daughter, as you have done so excellently. But for the rest, I intend to be the only master in my own house, and the only master of my child." She laid a hand upon my arm: "I implore you, Monsieur, don't do this!" Her fixed look did not leave my face, and seemed to be questioning me to the very bottom of my soul. "I have never believed it," she murmured, "No! I

236

never could believe it. But if you take the child away I shall."

"Believe what, wretched woman ? believe what ? "

Her voice sank lower still. "Believe that you knew how her mother came by her death ; and that you mean the daughter to die as she did."

"Die as her mother did ? "

"Yes ! by the same hand ! "

The sweat came on my forehead. I felt as it were a breathing of death upon me. But still I thrust away from me that terrible light on things.

"Victoire ! " I said, "take care ! You are no fool : you are something worse. Your hatred of the woman who has taken the place of my first wife—your blind hatred—has suggested to you odious, nay ! criminal words."

"Ah ! Ah ! Monsieur ! " she cried with wild energy. "After what I have just told you, take your daughter to live with that woman if you dare."

I walked up and down the room awhile to collect my senses. Then, returning to the old woman, "Yet how can I believe you ? " I asked. "If you had had the shadow of a proof of what you give me to understand, how could you have kept silence so long ? How could you have allowed me to contract that hateful marriage ? "

She seemed more confident, and her voice grew gentler. "Monsieur, it is because Madame, before she went to God, made me take oath on the crucifix to keep that secret for ever."

"Yet not with me, in fact,—not with me ! " And I, in turn, questioned her ; my eyes upon hers. She hesitated : then stammered out, "True ! not with you ! because she believed, poor little soul ! that . . ."

"What did she believe ? That I knew it ? That I was an accomplice ? Tell me ! " Her eyes fell, and she made no answer. "Is it possible, my God, is it possible ? But come, sit by me here, and tell me all you know, all you saw. At what time was it you noticed anything—the precise moment ? " For in truth she had been suffering for a long time past.

Victoire tells the miserable story of Sabine's

APPRECIATIONS

crime—we must pardon what we think a not quite worthy addition to the imaginary world M. Feuillet has called up round about him, for the sake of fully knowing Bernard and Aliette. The old nurse had surprised her in the very act, and did not credit her explanation. " When I surprised her," she goes on :

" It may already have been too late—be sure it was not the first time she had been guilty—my first thought was to give you information. But I had not the courage. Then I told Madame. I thought I saw plainly that I had nothing to tell she was not already aware of. Nevertheless she chided me almost harshly. 'You know very well,' she said, 'that my husband is always there when Mademoiselle prepares the medicines. So that he too would be guilty. Rather than believe that, I would accept death at his hands a hundred times over !' And I remember, Monsieur, how at the very moment when she told me that, you came out from the little *boudoir*, and brought her a glass of valerian. She cast on me a terrible look and drank. A few minutes afterwards she was so ill that she thought the end was come. She begged me to give her her crucifix, and made me swear never to utter a word concerning our suspicions. It was then I sent for the priest. I have told you, Monsieur, what I know ; what I have seen with my own eyes. I swear that I have said nothing but what is absolutely true." She paused. I could not answer her. I seized her old wrinkled and trembling hands and pressed them to my forehead, and wept like a child.

May 10.—She died believing me guilty ! The thought is terrible to me. I know not what to do. A creature so frail, so delicate, so sweet. " Yes ! " she said to herself, " my husband is a murderer ; what he is giving me is poison, and he knows it." She died with that thought in her mind—her last thought. And she will never, never know that it was not so ; that I am innocent ; that the thought is torment to me : that I am the most unhappy of men. Ah ! God, all-powerful ! if you indeed exist, you see what I suffer. Have pity on me !

Ah ! how I wish I could believe that all is not over between

238

her and me ; that she sees and hears me ; that she knew the
truth. But I find it impossible ! impossible !

June.—That I was a criminal was her last thought, and
she will never be undeceived.

All seems so completely ended when one dies. All returns
to its first elements. How credit that miracle of a personal
resurrection ? and yet in truth all is mystery,—miracle, around
us, about us, within ourselves. The entire universe is but a
continuous miracle. Man's new birth from the womb of death
—is it a mystery less comprehensible than his birth from the
womb of his mother ?

Those lines are the last written by Bernard de Vaudricourt. His health, for some time past disturbed by grief, was
powerless against the emotions of the last terrible trial imposed
on him. A malady, the exact nature of which was not determined, in a few days assumed a mortal character. Perceiving
that his end was come, he caused Monseigneur de Courteheuse
to be summoned,—he desired to die in the religion of Aliette.
Living, the poor child had been defeated : she prevailed in her
death.

Two distinguished souls ! *deux êtres d'élite*—
M. Feuillet thinks—whose fine qualities properly
brought them together. When Mademoiselle
de Courteheuse said of the heroes of her favourite
age, that their passions, their errors, did but pass
over a ground of what was solid and serious,
and which always discovered itself afresh, she
was unconsciously describing Bernard. Singular
young brother of Monsieur de Camors—after
all, certainly, more fortunate than he—he belongs
to the age, which, if it had great faults, had also
great repentances. In appearance, frivolous ;
with all the light charm of the world, yet with
that impressibility to great things, according to
the law which makes the best of M. Feuillet's

APPRECIATIONS

characters so interesting ; above all, with that capacity for pity which almost everything around him tended to suppress ; in real life, if he exists there, and certainly in M. Feuillet's pages, it is a refreshment to meet him.

1886.

POSTSCRIPT

αἰνεῖ δὲ παλαιὸν μὲν οἶνον, ἄνθεα δ᾽ ὕμνων νεωτέρων

THE words, *classical* and *romantic*, although, like
many other critical expressions, sometimes abused
by those who have understood them too vaguely
or too absolutely, yet define two real tendencies
in the history of art and literature.   Used in an
exaggerated sense, to express a greater opposition
between those tendencies than really exists, they
have at times tended to divide people of taste
into opposite camps.   But in that *House Beautiful*,
which the creative minds of all generations—
the artists and those who have treated life in the
spirit of art—are always building together, for
the refreshment of the human spirit, these op-
positions cease ; and the *Interpreter* of the *House
Beautiful*, the true æsthetic critic, uses these
divisions, only so far as they enable him to enter
into the peculiarities of the objects with which
he has to do.   The term *classical*, fixed, as it is,
to a well-defined literature, and a well-defined
group in art, is clear, indeed ; but then it has
often been used in a hard, and merely scholastic

P. V   241   R

sense, by the praisers of what is old and accustomed, at the expense of what is new, by critics who would never have discovered for themselves the charm of any work, whether new or old, who value what is old, in art or literature, for its accessories, and chiefly for the conventional authority that has gathered about it—people who would never really have been made glad by any Venus fresh-risen from the sea, and who praise the Venus of old Greece and Rome, only because they fancy her grown now into something staid and tame.

And as the term, *classical*, has been used in a too absolute, and therefore in a misleading sense, so the term, *romantic*, has been used much too vaguely, in various accidental senses. The sense in which Scott is called a romantic writer is chiefly this ; that, in opposition to the literary tradition of the last century, he loved strange adventure, and sought it in the Middle Age. Much later, in a Yorkshire village, the spirit of romanticism bore a more really characteristic fruit in the work of a young girl, Emily Brontë, the romance of *Wuthering Heights ;* the figures of Hareton Earnshaw, of Catherine Linton, and of Heathcliffe—tearing open Catherine's grave, removing one side of her coffin, that he may really lie beside her in death—figures so passionate, yet woven on a background of delicately beautiful, moorland scenery, being typical examples of that spirit. In Germany, again, that spirit is shown less in Tieck, its professional representative, than in Meinhold, the author of *Sidonia the Sorceress* and the *Amber-Witch*. In Germany and France, within the last hundred years, the term has been used to describe a particular school of writers ; and, consequently, when Heine criticises the *Romantic School* in Germany—that movement which culminated in Goethe's *Goetz von Berlichingen ;* or when Théophile Gautier criticises the romantic movement in France, where, indeed, it bore its most characteristic fruits, and its play is hardly yet over where, by a certain audacity, or *bizarrerie* of motive, united with faultless literary execution, it still shows itself in imaginative literature, they use the word, with an exact sense of special artistic qualities, indeed ; but use it, nevertheless, with a limited application to the manifestation of those qualities at a particular period. But the romantic spirit is, in reality, an ever-present, an enduring principle, in the artistic temperament ; and the qualities of thought and style which that, and other similar uses of the word *romantic* really indicate, are indeed but symptoms of a very continuous and widely working influence.

Though the words *classical* and *romantic*, then, have acquired an almost technical meaning, in application to certain developments of German and French taste, yet this is but one variation of an old opposition, which may be traced from the

very beginning of the formation of European art
and literature. From the first formation of anything like a standard of taste in these things,
the restless curiosity of their more eager lovers
necessarily made itself felt, in the craving for new
motives, new subjects of interest, new modifications of style. Hence, the opposition between
the classicists and the romanticists—between the
adherents, in the culture of beauty, of the
principles of liberty, and authority, respectively
—of strength, and order or what the Greeks
called κοσμιότης.

Sainte-Beuve, in the third volume of the
Causeries du Lundi, has discussed the question,
What is meant by a classic? It was a question he
was well fitted to answer, having himself lived
through many phases of taste, and having been
in earlier life an enthusiastic member of the
romantic school : he was also a great master of
that sort of " philosophy of literature," which
delights in tracing traditions in it, and the
way in which various phases of thought and
sentiment maintain themselves, through successive modifications, from epoch to epoch.
His aim, then, is to give the word *classic* a
wider and, as he says, a more generous sense
than it commonly bears, to make it expressly
grandiose et flottant; and, in doing this, he
develops, in a masterly manner, those qualities
of measure, purity, temperance, of which it
is the especial function of classical art

and literature, whatever meaning, narrower or wider, we attach to the term, to take care.

The charm, therefore, of what is classical, in art or literature, is that of the well-known tale, to which we can, nevertheless, listen over and over again, because it is told so well. To the absolute beauty of its artistic form, is added the accidental, tranquil, charm of familiarity. There are times, indeed, at which these charms fail to work on our spirits at all, because they fail to excite us. " *Romanticism,*" says Stendhal, " is the art of presenting to people the literary works which, in the actual state of their habits and beliefs, are capable of giving them the greatest possible pleasure ; *classicism,* on the contrary, of presenting them with that which gave the greatest possible pleasure to their grandfathers." But then, beneath all changes of habits and beliefs, our love of that mere abstract proportion—of music—which what is classical in literature possesses, still maintains itself in the best of us, and what pleased our grandparents may at least tranquillise us. The " classic " comes to us out of the cool and quiet of other times, as the measure of what a long experience has shown will at least never displease us. And in the classical literature of Greece and Rome, as in the classics of the last century, the essentially classical element is that quality of order in beauty, which they possess, indeed, in a pre-eminent degree, and which impresses some minds to the exclusion of everything else in them.

It is the addition of strangeness to beauty, that constitutes the romantic character in art ; and the desire of beauty being a fixed element in every artistic organisation, it is the addition of curiosity to this desire of beauty, that constitutes the romantic temper. Curiosity and the desire of beauty, have each their place in art, as in all true criticism. When one's curiosity is deficient, when one is not eager enough for new impressions, and new pleasures, one is liable to value mere academical proprieties too highly, to be satisfied with worn-out or conventional types, with the insipid ornament of Racine, or the prettiness of that later Greek sculpture, which passed so long for true Hellenic work ; to miss those places where the handiwork of nature, or of the artist, has been most cunning ; to find the most stimulating products of art a mere irritation. And when one's curiosity is in excess, when it overbalances the desire of beauty, then one is liable to value in works of art what is inartistic in them ; to be satisfied with what is exaggerated in art, with productions like some of those of the romantic school in Germany ; not to distinguish, jealously enough, between what is admirably done, and what is done not quite so well, in the writings, for instance, of Jean Paul. And if I had to give

instances of these defects, then I should say, that
Pope, in common with the age of literature to
which he belonged, had too little curiosity, so
that there is always a certain insipidity in the
effect of his work, exquisite as it is ; and,
coming down to our own time, that Balzac
had an excess of curiosity—curiosity not duly
tempered with the desire of beauty.

But, however falsely those two tendencies
may be opposed by critics, or exaggerated by
artists themselves, they are tendencies really at
work at all times in art, moulding it, with the
balance sometimes a little on one side, sometimes
a little on the other, generating, respectively, as
the balance inclines on this side or that, two
principles, two traditions, in art, and in literature
so far as it partakes of the spirit of art. If
there is a great overbalance of curiosity, then,
we have the grotesque in art : if the union of
strangeness and beauty, under very difficult and
complex conditions, be a successful one, if the
union be entire, then the resultant beauty is
very exquisite, very attractive. With a passionate
care for beauty, the romantic spirit refuses to
have it, unless the condition of strangeness be
first fulfilled. Its desire is for a beauty born of
unlikely elements, by a profound alchemy, by a
difficult initiation, by the charm which wrings it
even out of terrible things ; and a trace of distortion, of the grotesque, may perhaps linger, as
an additional element of expression, about its

ultimate grace. Its eager, excited spirit will
have strength, the grotesque, first of all—the
trees shrieking as you tear off the leaves ; for
Jean Valjean, the long years of convict life ; for
Redgauntlet, the quicksands of Solway Moss ;
then, incorporate with this strangeness, and
intensified by restraint, as much sweetness, as
much beauty, as is compatible with that.
Énergique, frais, et dispos—these, according to
Sainte-Beuve, are the characteristics of a genuine
classic—*les ouvrages anciens ne sont pas classiques
parce qu'ils sont vieux, mais parce qu'ils sont
énergiques, frais, et dispos.* Energy, freshness,
intelligent and masterly disposition :—these are
characteristics of Victor Hugo when his alchemy
is complete, in certain figures, like Marius and
Cosette, in certain scenes, like that in the
opening of *Les Travailleurs de la Mer*, where
Déruchette writes the name of *Gilliatt* in the
snow, on Christmas morning ; but always there
is a certain note of strangeness discernible there,
as well.

The essential elements, then, of the romantic
spirit are curiosity and the love of beauty ; and
it is only as an illustration of these qualities, that
it seeks the Middle Age, because, in the over-
charged atmosphere of the Middle Age, there
are unworked sources of romantic effect, of a
strange beauty, to be won, by strong imagination,
out of things unlikely or remote.

Few, probably, now read Madame de Staël's

POSTSCRIPT

De l'Allemagne, though it has its interest, the interest which never quite fades out of work really touched with the enthusiasm of the spiritual adventurer, the pioneer in culture. It was published in 1810, to introduce to French readers a new school of writers—the romantic school, from beyond the Rhine ; and it was followed, twenty-three years later, by Heine's *Romantische Schule,* as at once a supplement and a correction. Both these books, then, connect romanticism with Germany, with the names especially of Goethe and Tieck ; and, to many English readers, the idea of romanticism is still inseparably connected with Germany—that Germany which, in its quaint old towns, under the spire of Strasburg or the towers of Heidelberg, was always listening in rapt inaction to the melodious, fascinating voices of the Middle Age, and which, now that it has got Strasburg back again, has, I suppose, almost ceased to exist. But neither Germany, with its Goethe and Tieck, nor England, with its Byron and Scott, is nearly so representative of the romantic temper as France, with Murger, and Gautier, and Victor Hugo. It is in French literature that its most characteristic expression is to be found ; and that, as most closely derivative, historically, from such peculiar conditions, as ever reinforce it to the utmost.

For, although temperament has much to do with the generation of the romantic spirit, and

although this spirit, with its curiosity, its thirst
for a curious beauty, may be always traceable in
excellent art (traceable even in Sophocles) yet
still, in a limited sense, it may be said to be a
product of special epochs. Outbreaks of this
spirit, that is, come naturally with particular
periods—times, when, in men's approaches
towards art and poetry, curiosity may be noticed
to take the lead, when men come to art and
poetry, with a deep thirst for intellectual
excitement, after a long *ennui*, or in reaction
against the strain of outward, practical things :
in the later Middle Age, for instance ; so that
medieval poetry, centering in Dante, is often
opposed to Greek and Roman poetry, as romantic
poetry to the classical. What the romanticism
of Dante is, may be estimated, if we compare
the lines in which Virgil describes the hazel-
wood, from whose broken twigs flows the blood
of Polydorus, not without the expression of a
real shudder at the ghastly incident, with the
whole canto of the *Inferno*, into which Dante
has expanded them, beautifying and softening it,
meanwhile, by a sentiment of profound pity.
And it is especially in that period of intellectual
disturbance, immediately preceding Dante, amid
which the romance languages define themselves
at last, that this temper is manifested. Here, in
the literature of Provence, the very name of
romanticism is stamped with its true signification :
here we have indeed a romantic world, grotesque

even, in the strength of its passions, almost insane in its curious expression of them, drawing all things into its sphere, making the birds, nay ! lifeless things, its voices and messengers, yet so penetrated with the desire for beauty and sweetness, that it begets a wholly new species of poetry, in which the *Renaissance* may be said to begin. The last century was pre-eminently a classical age, an age in which, for art and literature, the element of a comely order was in the ascendant ; which, passing away, left a hard battle to be fought between the classical and the romantic schools. Yet, it is in the heart of this century, of Goldsmith and Stothard, of Watteau and the *Siècle de Louis XIV.*—in one of its central, if not most characteristic figures, in Rousseau— that the modern or French romanticism really originates. But, what in the eighteenth century is but an exceptional phenomenon, breaking through its fair reserve and discretion only at rare intervals, is the habitual guise of the nineteenth, breaking through it perpetually, with a feverishness, an incomprehensible straining and excitement, which all experience to some degree, but yearning also, in the genuine children of the romantic school, to be *énergique, frais, et dispos*— for those qualities of energy, freshness, comely order ; and often, in Murger, in Gautier, in Victor Hugo, for instance, with singular felicity attaining them.

It is in the terrible tragedy of Rousseau, in

APPRECIATIONS

fact, that French romanticism, with much else, begins : reading his *Confessions* we seem actually to assist at the birth of this new, strong spirit in the French mind. The wildness which has shocked so many, and the fascination which has influenced almost every one, in the squalid, yet eloquent figure, we see and hear so clearly in that book, wandering under the apple-blossoms and among the vines of Neuchâtel or Vevey actually give it the quality of a very successful romantic invention. His strangeness or distortion, his profound subjectivity, his passionateness—the *cor laceratum*—Rousseau makes all men in love with these. *Je ne suis fait comme aucun de ceux que j'ai sus. Mais si je ne vaux pas mieux, au moins je suis autre.*—"I am not made like any one else I have ever known : yet, if I am not better, at least I am different." These words, from the first page of the *Confessions*, anticipate all the Werthers, Renés, Obermanns, of the last hundred years. For Rousseau did but anticipate a trouble in the spirit of the whole world ; and thirty years afterwards, what in him was a peculiarity, became part of the general consciousness. A storm was coming : Rousseau, with others, felt it in the air, and they helped to bring it down : they introduced a disturbing element into French literature, then so trim and formal, like our own literature of the age of Queen Anne.

In 1815 the storm had come and gone, but had left, in the spirit of "young France," the *ennui* of an immense disillusion. In the last chapter of Edgar Quinet's *Révolution Française*, a work itself full of irony, of disillusion, he distinguishes two books, Senancour's *Obermann* and Chateaubriand's *Génie du Christianisme*, as characteristic of the first decade of the present century. In those two books we detect already the disease and the cure—in *Obermann* the irony, refined into a plaintive philosophy of " indifference "—in Chateaubriand's *Génie du Christianisme*, the refuge from a tarnished actual present, a present of disillusion, into a world of strength and beauty in the Middle Age, as at an earlier period—in *René* and *Atala*—into the free play of them in savage life. It is to minds in this spiritual situation, weary of the present, but yearning for the spectacle of beauty and strength, that the works of French romanticism appeal. They set a positive value on the intense, the exceptional ; and a certain distortion is sometimes noticeable in them, as in conceptions like Victor Hugo's *Quasimodo*, or *Gwynplaine*, something of a terrible grotesque, of the *macabre*, as the French themselves call it ; though always combined with perfect literary execution, as in Gautier's *La Morte Amoureuse*, or the scene of the " maimed " burial-rites of the player, dead of the frost, in his *Capitaine Fracasse*—true " flowers of the yew." It becomes grim humour in Victor Hugo's combat of Gilliatt with the devil-fish, or the incident, with all its ghastly comedy drawn

out at length, of the great gun detached from
its fastenings on shipboard, in *Quatre-Vingt-Trieze*
(perhaps the most terrible of all the accidents
that can happen by sea) and in the entire episode,
in that book, of the *Convention*. Not less surely
does it reach a genuine pathos ; for the habit
of noting and distinguishing one's own most
intimate passages of sentiment makes one
sympathetic, begetting, as it must, the power
of entering, by all sorts of finer ways, into the
intimate recesses of other minds ; so that pity
is another quality of romanticism, both Victor
Hugo and Gautier being great lovers of animals,
and charming writers about them, and Murger
being unrivalled in the pathos of his *Scènes de la
Vie de Jeunesse*. Penetrating so finely into all
situations which appeal to pity, above all, into
the special or exceptional phases of such feeling, the romantic humour is not afraid of the
quaintness or singularity of its circumstances or
expression, pity, indeed, being of the essence
of humour ; so that Victor Hugo does but turn
his romanticism into practice, in his hunger and
thirst after practical *Justice !*—a justice which
shall no longer wrong children, or animals, for
instance, by ignoring in a stupid, mere breadth
of view, minute facts about them. Yet the
romanticists are antinomian, too, sometimes,
because the love of energy and beauty, of
distinction in passion, tended naturally to
become a little *bizarre*, plunging into the

POSTSCRIPT

Middle Age, into the secrets of old Italian story. *Are we in the Inferno ?*—we are tempted to ask, wondering at something malign in so much beauty. For over all a care for the refreshment of the human spirit by fine art manifests itself, a predominant sense of literary charm, so that, in their search for the secret of exquisite expression, the romantic school went back to the forgotten world of early French poetry, and literature itself became the most delicate of the arts—like " goldsmith's work," says Sainte-Beuve, of Bertrand's *Gaspard de la Nuit*—and that peculiarly French gift, the gift of exquisite speech, *argute loqui*, attained in them a perfection which it had never seen before.

Stendhal, a writer whom I have already quoted, and of whom English readers might well know much more than they do, stands between the earlier and later growths of the romantic spirit. His novels are rich in romantic quality ; and his other writings—partly criticism, partly personal reminiscences—are a very curious and interesting illustration of the needs out of which romanticism arose. In his book on *Racine and Shakespeare*, Stendhal argues that all good art was romantic in its day ; and this is perhaps true in Stendhal's sense. That little treatise, full of " dry light " and fertile ideas, was published in the year 1823, and its object is to defend an entire independence and liberty in the choice and treatment of subject, both in art and literature, against those who upheld the exclusive authority of precedent. In pleading the cause of romanticism, therefore, it is the novelty, both of form and of motive, in writings like the *Hernani* of Victor Hugo (which soon followed it, raising a storm of criticism) that he is chiefly concerned to justify. To be interesting and really stimulating, to keep us from yawning even, art and literature must follow the subtle movements of that nimbly-shifting *Time-Spirit*, or *Zeit-Geist*, understood by French not less than by German criticism, which is always modifying men's taste, as it modifies their manners and their pleasures. This, he contends, is what all great workmen had always understood. Dante, Shakespeare, Molière, had exercised an absolute independence in their choice of subject and treatment. To turn always with that ever-changing spirit, yet to retain the flavour of what was admirably done in past generations, in the classics, as we say —is the problem of true romanticism. "Dante," he observes, "was pre-eminently the romantic poet. He adored Virgil, yet he wrote the *Divine Comedy*, with the episode of Ugolino, which is as unlike the *Æneid* as can possibly be. And those who thus obey the fundamental principle of romanticism, one by one become classical, and are joined to that ever-increasing common league, formed by men of all countries, to approach nearer and nearer to perfection."

Romanticism, then, although it has its epochs,

POSTSCRIPT

is in its essential characteristics rather a spirit which shows itself at all times, in various degrees, in individual workmen and their work, and the amount of which criticism has to estimate in them taken one by one, than the peculiarity of a time or a school. Depending on the varying proportion of curiosity and the desire of beauty, natural tendencies of the artistic spirit at all times, it must always be partly a matter of individual temperament. The eighteenth century in England has been regarded as almost exclusively a classical period ; yet William Blake, a type of so much which breaks through what are conventionally thought the influences of that century, is still a noticeable phenomenon in it, and the reaction in favour of naturalism in poetry begins in that century, early. There are, thus, the born romanticists and the born classicists. There are the born classicists who start with *form*, to whose minds the comeliness of the old, immemorial, well-recognised types in art and literature, have revealed themselves impressively ; who will entertain no matter which will not go easily and flexibly into them ; whose work aspires only to be a variation upon, or study from, the older masters. " 'Tis art's decline, my son !" they are always saying, to the progressive element in their own generation ; to those who care for that which in fifty years' time every one will be caring for. On the other hand, there are the born romanticists, who start with an original, untried *matter*, still in fusion ; who conceive this vividly, and hold by it as the essence of their work ; who, by the very vividness and heat of their conception, purge away, sooner or later, all that is not organically appropriate to it, till the whole effect adjusts itself in clear, orderly, proportionate form ; which form, after a very little time, becomes classical in its turn.

The romantic or classical character of a picture, a poem, a literary work, depends, then, on the balance of certain qualities in it ; and in this sense, a very real distinction may be drawn between good classical and good romantic work. But all critical terms are relative ; and there is at least a valuable suggestion in that theory of Stendhal's, that all good art was romantic in its day. In the beauties of Homer and Pheidias, quiet as they now seem, there must have been, for those who confronted them for the first time, excitement and surprise, the sudden, unforeseen satisfaction of the desire of beauty. Yet the *Odyssey*, with its marvellous adventure, is more romantic than the *Iliad*, which nevertheless contains, among many other romantic episodes, that of the immortal horses of Achilles, who weep at the death of Patroclus. Æschylus is more romantic than Sophocles, whose *Philoctetes*, were it written now, might figure, for the strangeness of its motive and the perfectness of its execution, as typically romantic ; while, of Euripides, it may be said, that his method in writing his plays is to sacrifice readily almost everything else, so that he may attain the fulness of a single romantic effect. These two tendencies, indeed, might be applied as a measure or standard, all through Greek and Roman art and poetry, with very illuminating results ; and for an analyst of the romantic principle in art, no exercise would be more profitable, than to walk through the collection of classical antiquities at the Louvre, or the British Museum, or to examine some representative collection of Greek coins, and note how the element of curiosity, of the love of strangeness, insinuates itself into classical design, and record the effects of the romantic spirit there, the traces of struggle, of the grotesque even, though over-balanced here by sweetness; as in the sculpture of Chartres and Rheims, the real sweetness of mind in the sculptor is often overbalanced by the grotesque, by the rudeness of his strength.

Classicism, then, means for Stendhal, for that younger enthusiastic band of French writers whose unconscious method he formulated into principles, the reign of what is pedantic, conventional, and narrowly academical in art ; for him, all good art is romantic. To Sainte-Beuve, who understands the term in a more liberal sense, it is the characteristic of certain epochs, of certain spirits in every epoch, not given to the exercise of original imagination, but rather to the working out of refinements of manner on some

APPRECIATIONS

authorised matter ; and who bring to their perfection, in this way, the elements of sanity, of
order and beauty in manner. In general criticism,
again, it means the spirit of Greece and Rome,
of some phases in literature and art that may
seem of equal authority with Greece and Rome,
the age of Louis the Fourteenth, the age of
Johnson ; though this is at best an uncritical use
of the term, because in Greek and Roman work
there are typical examples of the romantic spirit.
But explain the terms as we may, in application
to particular epochs, there are these two elements
always recognisable ; united in perfect art—in
Sophocles, in Dante, in the highest work of
Goethe, though not always absolutely balanced
there ; and these two elements may be not in-
appropriately termed the classical and romantic
tendencies.

Material for the artist, motives of inspiration,
are not yet exhausted : our curious, complex,
aspiring age still abounds in subjects for æsthetic
manipulation by the literary as well as by other
forms of art. For the literary art, at all events,
the problem just now is, to induce order upon
the contorted, proportionless accumulation of our
knowledge and experience, our science and history,
our hopes and disillusion, and, in effecting this,
to do consciously what has been done hitherto
for the most part too unconsciously, to write our
English language as the Latins wrote theirs, as the

POSTSCRIPT

French write, as scholars should write. Appealing, as he may, to precedent in this matter, the scholar will still remember that if " the style is the man " it is also the age : that the nineteenth century too will be found to have had its style, justified by necessity—a style very different, alike from the baldness of an impossible " Queen Anne " revival, and an incorrect, incondite exuberance, after the mode of Elizabeth : that we can only return to either at the price of an impoverishment of form or matter, or both, although, an intellectually rich age such as ours being necessarily an eclectic one, we may well cultivate some of the excellences of literary types so different as those : that in literature as in other matters it is well to unite as many diverse elements as may be : that the individual writer or artist, certainly, is to be estimated by the number of graces he combines, and his power of interpenetrating them in a given work. To discriminate schools, of art, of literature, is, of course, part of the obvious business of literary criticism : but, in the work of literary production, it is easy to be overmuch occupied concerning them. For, in truth, the legitimate contention is, not of one age or school of literary art against another, but of all successive schools alike, against the stupidity which is dead to the substance, and the vulgarity which is dead to form.